HOW TO TELL A TRUE STORY

HOW TO TELL A TRUE STORY

TRICIA SPRINGSTUBB

Margaret Ferguson Books
Holiday House · New York

Margaret Ferguson Books
An imprint of Holiday House Publishing, Inc.

Copyright © 2025 by Tricia Springstubb
All Rights Reserved
HOLIDAY HOUSE is registered in the U.S. Patent and Trademark Office.
Printed and bound in February 2025 at Sheridan, Chelsea, MI, USA.
www.holidayhouse.com
First Edition
1 3 5 7 9 10 8 6 4 2

Library of Congress Cataloging-in-Publication Data

Names: Springstubb, Tricia, author.
Title: How to tell a true story / Tricia Springstubb.
Description: First edition. | New York : Holiday House, 2025.
"Margaret Ferguson Books." | Audience term: Preteens
Audience: Ages 10–14. | Audience: Grades 4–6.
Summary: "After 7th grader Amber Price's secretive
older brother rescues her from a devastating house fire,
the community's response proves that kindness is as
complicated as family"— Provided by publisher.
Identifiers: LCCN 2024017543 | ISBN 9780823458486 (hardcover)
Subjects: CYAC: Family problems—Fiction. | Secrets—Fiction.
Fire—Fiction. | Conduct of life—Fiction. | LCGFT: Novels.
Classification: LCC PZ7.S76847 Ho 2025 | DDC [Fic]—dc23
LC record available at https://lccn.loc.gov/2024017543

ISBN: 978-0-8234-5848-6 (hardcover)

EU Authorized Representative: HackettFlynn Ltd, 36 Cloch Choirneal,
Balrothery, Co. Dublin, K32 C942, Ireland.
EU@walkerpublishinggroup.com

For my beautiful girls, Zoe, Phoebe, and Delia—true love now and forever

That Night

When Amber thought back to that night, everything seemed so normal. Dad working late, Mom sipping tea. School backpacks hooked over kitchen chairs. The blue casserole dish with dark streaks where the mac 'n' cheese had bubbled over. Goofy little Clancy talking about how some of her classmates made bad choices.

"Not me!" Clancy rocked her loose front tooth like a tiny drawbridge. "I do everything utterly perfect."

"Everything?" Their big brother, Gage, grinned. "That's utterly impossible."

That night, Gage was home. This was where he was supposed to be, since he was grounded (again). But lately he kept managing to find excuses to go out. Basketball practice, shifts at the Convenient Mart, study group (as if). If Dad had been around more, Gage would never have gotten away with it.

If Dad had been around more. Afterward, Amber thought about that, too.

Gage was three years older than she was. When they were little, he'd been the boss of her, but when she was finally old enough and he was still young enough, they'd become buddies.

Ride-scooters-make-hideouts-invent-secret-languages best buddies.

Those days were over. Gage was in high school now. He had his own private life, and it was getting privater by the minute.

Except *that* night, he was acting like a candidate for world's best family member. Before dinner, he'd helped Clancy clean out Iggy the Hamster's stinky cage, a true labor of love. He'd gone down to the basement and brought up the laundry—everybody's, not just his. And when the casserole dripped in the oven and set off the smoke detector, he'd climbed on a chair and taken out the battery without Mom even asking.

He was acting so sweet! Everything was so peaceful! When Amber thought back on that night, it was like looking at old photos where you sort of recognize your younger self but mostly you wonder *Who is that person? How can that be* me?

Gage shoveled in more mac 'n' cheese, and Amber began to hope he'd stay home all night. They'd hang out together, like ye olden days. They'd battle in *Segue III* or trade favorite video clips. If Gage stayed home, she'd even go out in the driveway and let him give her pointers on shooting hoops, though she found anything involving balls pointless.

"Gager," she said, his old nickname. He looked up with that grin.

"Amberghini."

Then his phone got a text.

Telepathy

That night, they were living in the new house.

Not *new* new. The house had creaky plumbing and peeling paint, and lots of people had lived in it before them. But it was new to the Price family and also a kind of miracle. Because they *owned* it.

For years, Dad had been on a home-buying mission. He worked extra shifts as an X-ray technician and pinched every penny till it yelped, all to save enough for a down payment. Dad was not a waver-y person. More like a the-shortest-distance-between-two-points-is-a-straight-line person. Gage knew better than to ask for the newest basketball shoes, and Amber never had the exact right jeans, because the Prices were saving, saving, always saving.

They'd moved in just two months ago. Now they lived in a house that needed tons of work, a house that used to be a rental and still had other people's left-behind junk in the basement and garage. But a house that belonged to them.

Scrimping wasn't over, though. Paying the mortgage, taxes, and insurance was a stretch. But the day they moved in, Mom made a banner that said OUR PRICE-LESS HOME and hung it over the mantel. And Dad, who was stingy with hugs, wrapped them all in his big, strong arms.

The not-new-but-new house was in the same neighborhood where they'd rented, so Amber could still walk to her middle school, to the thrift shop or library or Koko's Bakery, where she and her friends loved the bubble tea. She had to share a room with Clancy, but Amber didn't mind that as much as she pretended she did. Gage had claimed the third-floor attic. Tonight, after he got the text, he ran up there and came back down wearing a clean tee and a dark green hoodie.

"Gotta hit the library." An eye roll, like *what a pain in the butt.*

Doubt flickered across their mother's face. Just a flicker, but Amber saw. She wished she hadn't, but she couldn't help it. It was a kind of curse, the way she was always noticing things that nobody else in her family did.

"Again?" Mom asked Gage. "You went last night."

"It's a massive project." At least Gage had the decency to blush. "In fact, we've got to go to the main library, not the branch."

Once upon a time, Amber and Gage were wizards of telepathy. They'd close their eyes, put their fingers in their ears (who knew why they did that), and send each other messages across rooms, through walls. Once when Amber was on the corner and got scared frozen stiff by a big dog running loose, she put her fingers in her ears and shut her eyes, which was practically an invitation to the dog to attack her, but Gage had shown up out of nowhere to walk her home.

Amber tried it now.

Stop lying, airhead. Stay home before you get caught!

When she opened her eyes, her brother was looking at her. Had he gotten the message? He fingered his ear, like he felt something there. But then he blinked. He zipped up his hoodie, said he'd jog to the library. He needed the workout. One of the guys with a driver's license would give him a ride home.

Amber pretended to have a coughing fit, and he pretended not to notice. She stuck out her tongue, such a pathetic gesture, and he ignored that too. But at the last minute, hand on the doorknob, he turned and flashed her a happy smile. Beyond happy, really.

Angry as she was at him, Amber couldn't help smiling back.

The door bumped shut behind him.

Amoeba

Amber really needed to do her homework. She was behind in math, and she had an essay due for ELA. Ugh and ugh.

Amber was not a star student. Actually, she was not a star anything. When they'd studied amoebas in science, her best friend Lottie said they were fascinating, and her other best friend Mariah was grossed out. Amber? She'd secretly related to the blob-ish little things. They looked like they were trying to figure out what shape to be, and she knew how that felt.

Math, for example. She'd let Lottie talk her into moving up a level so they'd be in the same class. Lottie had sworn Amber could handle it. Amber just needed to have more confidence in herself! Lottie promised to help, and she tried—Lottie always kept her promises. But tonight's homework was about rational and irrational numbers and really, it all seemed irrational to Amber. She pushed her math book aside to help Clancy work on her habitat diorama. There was sugar snow and a musk ox, made from a little toy cow and brown hair clipped off an old Barbie doll. For unknown reasons, Clancy had fallen in love with musk ox.

"Mrs. Song will utterly flip when she sees this," Clancy said. "She'll say, 'It is perfect, just like you, Clancy Price.'"

Later, cleaning up, Amber noticed the smoke detector, still gaping like an empty shell. The battery lay on the counter. She could climb up and replace it, but really, why should she? Gage was the one who'd taken it out. He was the one who should put it back.

Upstairs, Mom was at her work table, a bright mess of silk flowers, colored paper, ribbons and tape and wire. It was October but she was working on her spring line of crafts, which she sold through an online store. She looked up, pushing back her long hair. Mom was so pretty, even with her nose smudged green from fabric paint. She was wearing Amber's favorite earrings, a gift from Dad: silver hoops with sparkly little stones.

"Bunnies, chicks, daffodils—here we go again!" When Mom shook her head, a pink feather drifted out of her hair. "Every year, the same old same old." She sighed. "Honestly. Sometimes I wonder what I'm doing."

"You're making stuff." Clancy tickled her with the feather, and Mom wrapped her in a hug.

"You're right as usual, Clance. Don't mind me." She kissed them both. "Sweet dreams, sweet daughters."

In the hallway, Clancy had to stop beside Mom and Dad's wedding photo. Dad was in his Army uniform and Mom wore a floaty dress she'd made. (Gage was in the photo, too, though you couldn't tell yet.) Dad stood arrow-straight while Mom leaned against him. They both looked dazzled, like they were squinting into a too-bright sun.

"Good night, Daddy." Clancy kissed her finger and pressed it to the glass.

Dad's shift at the urgent care ended at eleven. It took him twenty-two minutes to get home, twenty-five if he didn't hit the green lights. Gage had better be home first or there would be fireworks. Dad expected a lot of them all, but for the last year he'd been on Gage's case over approximately everything. Scraping by in school, being benched 99.9 percent of the time in basketball, having slacker friends. Gage needed to stand up straighter. He needed to speak up instead of mumble, and don't forget eye contact! He should quit wearing hoodies, which made him look like a shifty punk.

Basically, according to their father, Gage needed to be an entirely different person.

Anyone could see how entirely unfair that was.

But just try standing up to Dad.

Like the Tundra Misses Trees

That night, that innocent, without-a-clue night, while Clancy snored like a tiny steam engine and Iggy the Hamster scampered around his sparkling-clean cage, Amber lay in bed group texting with Lottie and Mariah. She and Lottie had known each other since first grade, and when Mariah moved here in fourth, they'd become a trio. An equilateral triangle, said Lottie, math genius. A hat trick, said Mariah, soccer superstar.

Now Mariah texted that she was destroyed by shooting drills, and Lottie said she had to help her stepmother, Rasheeda, take off her shoes, which was a real thing when you were seven months pregnant, not to mention if she didn't practice her viola, Mr. Halliday, the orchestra teacher, was going to take away her solo.

Miss u like the tundra misses trees. That was how they ended all their texts.

Amber stretched her legs and pointed her toes, a habit from when she was younger and thought she could make herself taller if only she tried. She was still one of the shortest kids in her class. She had straight hair that Mariah kindly called "sandy blond" and a sprinkle of pale freckles across her nose. In the crowded middle school halls, she was basically invisible.

Now she did some random scrolling. Kelly B., most popular of all the seventh-grade Kellys, had posted clips of her and her friends fooling around at an arcade. Someone who from the back looked like Mariah, but couldn't be, was there, and so was Lucas. He was playing pinball, arms stiff, face adorable with concentration. Lucas never posted anything himself, but he was always showing up in other people's feeds. Aack! There he was getting a one-arm hug from Mei, a Kelly B. wannabe. Amber clicked off.

The popular kids! It was easy to hate on them, but honestly, who wouldn't want to be one of them? Amber and her friends talked about it sometimes. Mariah said if they ever got popular, they'd be the nice variety, friends to all. Lottie said being popular was so outside her realm of being, it was easier to imagine being a narwhal. Amber said well, as long as they stuck together, they'd never be outcasts, which Lottie said was a pretty low bar, which made them all laugh because really? Popularity was a mystery.

Lucas had been wearing that cream-colored tee, the one that turned his dark brown eyes even darker. (Amber had more or less memorized all his clothes.)

By now it was nine thirty. The library closed at nine, so unless Gage's supposed friend with a supposed license had run out of gas or gotten a flat tire, Gage should be home by now.

Amber texted her brother.

Gage Price = wad of used gum.

No reply.

When Dad got angry with Gage, Mom tried to make peace, which almost never worked and usually made Dad angry at Mom, too. Around here, anger was a rolling snowball.

Come home, butthead!

No reply.

Amber slipped out of bed and down the hall. Her mother still sat at her table, but she wasn't working anymore. Chin on fist, she was staring out the window. Dad was at the urgent care, and Gage was somewhere he was not supposed to be. Amber thought of those dizzy little bugs she sometimes saw in a shaft of summer light, each one doing its own dance without even noticing the others all around it.

She almost went back to snuggle with Clancy, a thing she still did when she was lonesome or had a bad dream. Instead, she found herself climbing the narrow stairs to Gage's room at the top of the house.

Truth and Beauty, Part 1

The third floor was a single room with a slanted ceiling and one narrow window. The boxes they hadn't unpacked, with labels like BABY CLOTHES and ART PROJECTS, were stored up here. Gage had carved out a space for himself near the window. His bed, his desk, his chest of drawers. It reminded Amber of the hideouts they'd made when they were little, pretending to be spies or escaped prisoners.

She slid her feet into a pair of his basketball shoes and shuffled around, remembering how they used to put Barbies or action figures into Dad's dress shoes and pretend they were limos or armored tanks. She picked up one of Gage's free weights and swung it over her head, nearly dislocating her arm. Going to the open window, she took a deep breath. It was October, but the air was mild. Her phone rang.

"Do you remember Irene Mosher?" Lottie asked.

Amber smiled. Lottie had zero use for small talk.

"Mean Irene?" Amber kicked off Gage's shoes and stretched out on his bed. "From kindergarten? She always pushed me off the swing."

"One time she told me my gray dress was ugly. It was my favorite dress and gray was my favorite color!"

"It still is."

"Correct. I went home crying and my mother—you know, she was still alive then—she told me there were two ways I could solve the problem. I could stop wearing the dress to school or I could ignore Irene. Cave or stand up for myself. I remember I cried even harder because I hated both choices."

"So what did you do?"

"I don't know. I just remember my mom and I had Mallomars and chocolate milk." Lottie almost never talked about her mother, who'd died when they were in second grade. Now she blurted, "Mariah keeps snubbing me."

"What?"

"Ever since she became an Eagle, she's different."

Their middle school had three grades—sixth, seventh, and eighth. In sixth grade, everyone was jumbled together, but in seventh, they were divided into two teams. Mariah was an Eagle while Lottie and Amber were Falcons. (Whose genius idea was it to name the teams after birds of prey? At least there were no Vultures.) Different classes, different lunch periods. Not good, extremely not good, but what could they do? They were cogs in the machine that was Cloverville Middle.

"Today she and Kelly B. were talking by the bad bathroom. When I said hi, she didn't even turn her head."

"Kelly B. takes up all the oxygen. Probably Mariah didn't hear."

"She heard. I got a minuscule finger wave and that was it."

"That's not acceptable."

"She's climbing the social staircase."

Amber did a silent groan. Sometimes Lottie was so—so *definite*. Maybe Mariah was more distant lately, but that was just circumstances. It wasn't like she'd turned *mean*.

Though now Amber remembered how, a few days ago, walking to school, Mariah had told Lottie please not to take this the wrong way, but had she ever considered going to a dermatologist? She said she'd been to one (this was news, because Mariah's skin was perfect) and it had really helped her self-esteem. When Lottie looked pained, Mariah didn't seem to notice, even though they all knew Lottie had issues with her looks.

And later, Lottie paused in the hallway outside home base, where their teacher had posted October's Words of Wisdom.

> *Beauty is truth, truth beauty,—that is all*
> *Ye know on earth, and all ye need to know.*
> —John Keats

"I guess I'm a lie then," Lottie had said.

"Ye are so bizarre," Amber had replied.

"That's why ye love me, right?"

"Ye are blocking the doorway." Lucas had tapped Amber on the shoulder.

Like she was a twig and he was a match. Like she was a gong and he was the—whatever you called that thing you struck a gong with. That was how Lucas being so close made Amber feel.

"Helloo? Amboo?" Lottie said now. "Are you there?"

Through the window came a dog's bark, music from a passing car.

"You need to talk to Mariah," she said. "Let her know she's hurting your feelings."

"Maybe."

"Meanwhile talk to me."

Amber pulled up Gage's comforter and they went on talking about this and that and this again. By now it was hard to keep her eyes open, and she snuggled into her brother's pillow, which really, truly needed a clean pillowcase.

Did she and Lottie ever say goodbye?

Fire

When she woke, it took a moment to remember where she was.

Swimming up through grogginess, she thought, Someone in the neighborhood has a campfire.

She thought, I should close the window, the smoke's getting in here.

She thought, Wildfires—they've been on the news all summer, racing across the land, devouring everything in their path.

But there were no forests around here.

When she opened her eyes, a gray wall rose in front of her. When she tried to touch it, her hand disappeared. Heat licked her palm and she yanked it back. Gage's room, that's where she was. Alone at the top of the house.

Sitting up, she began to cough. The smoke—it was getting inside her. Her throat clogged with it and she coughed again, trying to get it out, but that hurt too much, so she closed her mouth and tried not to breathe. She swung her feet over the side of the bed, yelped and jerked them back. The floor burned like asphalt in summer. Like that time she and Mariah dared each other to go barefoot across the mall parking lot and wound up howling and hopping and had to give up.

A pair of Gage's socks lay on the floor beside the bed and she pulled them on, then stood up. From downstairs came a creaking sound, like a tree in a high wind, then a crash.

Her house was on fire. Her house was on fire! She had to get out.

But first she had to breathe. Going to the window, she pressed her face against the screen and gulped down clean air. Black smoke billowed out the window below. Her parents' room.

"Mom!" she screamed. "Clancy!"

Did someone answer? The fire made so much noise, she couldn't be sure. Were they awake? Were they all right? She tried to see the yard below, praying they were out there, but smoke whirled up, blocking her view. Amber pushed on the screen with both hands, but it didn't give. The heat at her back screamed *Get out*. It hollered *Jump*.

Wait. A fire escape ladder—didn't Dad buy one to keep up here? She spun back to the room. If there was a ladder, who knew where it was? Gage probably had never even unpacked it. The air was thicker now, tiny gritty things stinging her eyes and catching on her tongue. She remembered a fireman visiting her first-grade class. She'd sat on the carpet, looking up at a man in a black uniform with scary reflective stripes, her heart beating much too fast as he intoned the words *stop drop and roll*. But wasn't that only if you personally were on fire? Still, she pulled a sheet off the bed, wrapped it around herself, and dropped to a crouch. For a long moment, she rested her cheek against the side of her brother's bed, trying to gather her courage. Another sock lay on the floor and she pulled it over one hand, then, squinting, barely able to see, forced herself to start crawling toward where she thought the stairs were. The sheet tangled. The boxes—she bumped her head against one, then another. They seemed to be everywhere she turned, popping up like demons in a video game. She tried not to breathe. She tried not to cry.

"Amber! Amber Jade!"

It was her mother's voice, but far away. Much too far away. Amber sat back on her heels. That was when it came to her. Nobody knew where she was.

"Mom! I'm in the attic!"

Fire needed oxygen to burn. One of the best ways to put it out was to smother it. But this fire was winning the smothering contest. It was gobbling up every atom of oxygen, leaving none for her.

"Mom!"

Her mother didn't answer. Or did she? Amber couldn't

tell. It was getting so noisy. So much crackling and popping and creaking. Lowering her head, she started crawling again. If she could just get to the top of the stairs. Or maybe she should go back to the window and get some air. All she wanted to do was breathe! But no—she needed—what did she need?

"Amber! Amber!"

For a second she didn't recognize the hoarse, terrified voice. But then he shouted again.

"Amber! Where are you?"

"Gage!" The word flew out like some tiny white bird sweeping through the clouds of smoke. "In your room!"

"I'm coming! Keep talking! Let me hear you!"

She said his name again. And again and again. It drew him to her, or her to him, or both. Afterward, all she could remember was that a path had magically opened in front of her. The boxes had moved, all by themselves, and she'd crawled to the top of the stairs where Gage appeared, ringed with light, wearing a crown of gold. She stumbled to her feet and threw her arms around his sooty, sweaty neck. She pressed her face against his chest, still saying his name, as he wrapped his hoodie around her and carried her down the steps, the walls of flame and smoke seeming to part, the fire bowing before them.

Gone

"Iggy the Hamster got insinuated." Clancy's voice floated above her.

"Incinerated," whispered Mom, and then, "Sweetie? Sweetie, are you waking up?"

"Our musk ox, too," Clancy said.

Amber opened her eyes. Her sister and mother stood beside the hospital bed. Poor Mom! She was getting swallowed by a boa constrictor! No, wait, it was a dress, a hideous brown-and-green dress much too big for her. Amber pushed herself up on her elbows. She'd been slipping in and out of sleep and each time she woke, she had to figure things out all over again. What had happened? What was real and what was the worst nightmare she'd ever had?

"Gage," she said, and her mother took her hands.

"He's going to be all right." Mom swallowed. "He has burns but he'll be all right, sweetie. And so will you."

Though she lay in a bed white as the winter tundra, though tubes were bringing her pure, clean air, Amber could still smell the fire. She could still taste the smoke. It was like the fire had come with her, like she'd carried it down the stairs of the house, across the blazing kitchen, out into the night. Leaning back, she remembered slivers of what had happened next: an ambulance ride, being wheeled on a gurney, a nice nurse with cat-eye glasses hooking her up to stuff while explaining they needed to monitor her lungs for smoke inhalation. Amber thought she remembered the nurse using the word *lucky*, though that must be wrong.

Mom's dress was so weird. Clancy wore something strange too—a T-shirt with a chessboard on it. Slowly at first, and then in a great flash, Amber understood. Their own clothes were gone.

Her brain did a short-circuit.

What else?

"Iggy went to hamster heaven." Clancy scrubbed her nose with Amber's sheet. "He has a golden wheel and gets to eat strawberries twenty-four-seven."

Little Iggy, scampering around his clean cage, no idea he was about to be... Amber gripped her mother's hand. What if they weren't telling the truth about Gage? What if they were just trying to make her feel better, when really...

"Mom! I need to see Gage."

"Oh, sweetie, I don't think that's a good idea. He's in a special unit for burns and—"

"Right now!" she cried. "I want to see him right now!"

"Okay, okay. I'll find a nurse and ask."

The nurse, whose name was Kevin, had long locs and a tattoo of vines and butterflies that twined around his biceps and disappeared up under his scrubs. He took Amber's pulse and temperature. He tested her oxygen level with that stapler-like thing, and when he was satisfied, he unhooked the IV and helped her into a wheelchair.

They took an elevator, then turned left down a long, wide corridor. Kevin pushed her past an alcove where some exhausted-looking visitors sat. They were all adults except for one girl with green-streaked hair, staring at a sketchbook on her lap. What could anyone find to draw in this totally anti-beautiful place?

Everyone working on Gage's floor wore masks, gowns, gloves. Infection, Kevin told them, was a major concern with burns. When they got to Gage's room, Dad was just coming out. He wore his own familiar work scrubs, and compared to everyone else, he looked so normal, so *before*, Amber started to cry.

"Amber, it's okay. You're safe." He peeled off his mask and knelt beside her. "No need to cry."

"I know. I just... I'm not..."

"You're getting your color back. That's a good sign." He pulled out a handkerchief (Dad used real handkerchiefs) and gently wiped her tears. "How do you feel?"

Sad lost so confused—Amber swallowed the words. Dad

was right. She was safe. Even though, if she closed her eyes for more than a second, she still saw the leaping flames. Taking a ragged breath, she tried to smile. She tried to say what her father wanted to hear.

"I feel better."

"That's my girl. That's my Lamber." He stood up and turned to Mom. "I've got to go to work."

"Now?" Mom took a step back. Her ugly dress slid around. "Please don't. Call off. They'll understand, Gus."

"They're really short-staffed this week. They need me."

"*They* need you?"

"Don't do this, Meg. You think I *want* to leave?" Dad's eyebrows drew together in a bushy clump. Dad kept his hair clipped close, but his eyebrows were out of control. When Mom didn't answer, he said, "If we're going to get through this, we need to keep a steady keel."

"Speak for yourself," Mom said.

Amber gripped the arms of her wheelchair. They wouldn't argue here, not now, would they? To her relief, Dad said goodbye and headed down the corridor, just as Kevin, who'd been checking on Gage, came out of his room.

"All right then." Kevin crossed his arms. "Normally on this unit it's two visitors at a time and no one under sixteen." He pulled a stern face. "I know I can trust Amber to behave. What about you, Clancy?"

"You can trust me utterly!" she said.

"Gage is on strong meds for the pain," Kevin told them. "He'll be a little woozy."

"We won't stay long," Mom said.

Kevin brought masks and gowns, and when Mom, Amber and Clancy were all germ-proofed, they went into Gage's room. For a moment, not counting the tubes and monitors, he looked like normal old Gage. Then Mom wheeled Amber closer to the bed and she saw the angry red blisters on the backs of his hands. His right arm, between the wrist and the elbow, was mummified in gauze. He looked at Amber with half-closed eyes, and her breath stuck in her throat.

"Does it hurt?" Clancy whispered.

"Like you know what," he whispered back.

"Like hell!" Clancy shouted.

"You got it."

He'd saved her. He'd wrapped her in his hoodie and she'd pressed her face to his chest, she'd felt his heart pounding and his arms shaking so that by the time they got to the first floor, she knew she'd been mistaken. There was no magic in him or her. He was just a boy, like she was just a girl. Yet he'd saved her. He'd guided her through the heat and noise, out into cool night air so delicious she'd wanted to drink it by the gallon, and now here she was, with only a few small first-degree burns while he...

"I'm sorry," Amber said. He didn't hear, or pretended not to, so she said it louder. "I'm sorry, Gage."

"What are you talking about?" He sounded like he'd swallowed pebbles.

It's all my fault! The words turned to smoke, clogging her throat, stinging her eyes. *If only I didn't go up to your room. If only I didn't fall asleep.* She started crying all over again. *If only!*

"Sweetie," Mom said. "Come on, you and Gage both need to rest."

Clancy whined that she didn't want to go, she wanted to stay, no she didn't, she hated the hospital, she hated everything, she hated the whole entire stupid world. She tripped on her gown, toppled over, and everything went to pieces till Kevin bustled in with a Dum-Dum lollipop that just happened to be Mystery Flavor, Clancy's favorite. Mom took her hand and Kevin turned Amber's wheelchair toward the door. When she twisted around to say goodbye, she and her brother locked eyes. His were wide open now, and the look in them made her skin prickle.

Gage, her brave-beyond-words brother, was scared.

What Would You Save?

Late that afternoon, Lottie and Mariah tiptoed into Amber's hospital room. They were arm in arm and Mariah clutched a big bouquet. At the foot of her bed, they froze, looking so freaked, Amber had to laugh.

"It's okay! I'm not going to die, I promise."

"Amboo bamboo! Omigod." Mariah rushed around the bed to grab Amber's un-IV hand. She was wearing that cute green jacket that looked so perfect with her dark red hair. Bright, tangy autumn air wafted off her—the outside world!

Lottie, wearing a plain gray tee and jeans, pulled up the only chair and perched to one side, leaving room for Mariah. But Mariah wasn't about to sit down.

"When I heard, I mean, I couldn't believe it, I almost still can't." She brushed a strand of Amber's hair off her cheek. "I am just so glad to see you!"

"Me too." The tears started coming and Amber bit the insides of her cheeks. She had to stop crying over every single thing!

"We'd have come earlier but of course our parents insisted we go to school." Mariah glanced at Lottie, who nodded. "And then we had to wait for my mom to get home, and Lot's stepmom to... oh never mind! Here we are!" She hugged Amber, crushing the bouquet.

"How do you feel, Amber?" Lottie took the bouquet and laid it on the chair. "That's a rhetorical question. Of course you feel awful."

"I'm much better now that you're here."

"Us too." Mariah sighed. "So many people asked about you."

"Wait," Amber said. "What?"

"It was on the morning news, and word spread like, well, I guess like fire. What Gage did! People can't believe it. In ELA, Mr. Patel let us talk about it for the whole period. Nobody else in the class knows you very well—I mean, they know who you are but that's all—so I described how we're best friends." She gathered her hair into a messy bun. "I told them how Gage was afraid of all kinds of things, including foul shots, oral reports, and tsunamis, even though the nearest ocean is like five hundred miles away. I said he was the last person I'd imagine being a superhero!"

"Amber." Lottie's voice was soft but serious. "How did it even happen?"

Did she mean how did Amber and Gage get out? Or how did the fire start? Or was she asking a bigger question, like how could something so terrible even happen at all?

It was the first time Amber told the story, and she fumbled for words. Mostly she repeated what her mother had told her. Mom woke up and smelled smoke. She ran to their bedroom and got Clancy, ran downstairs to look for Amber but didn't find her, took Clancy outside and ran back in, though by now the smoke and heat made her dizzy. Out of nowhere Gage appeared, yelling at her to get out as he charged up the stairs.

Lottie looked somber but Mariah's eyes went round as if she were watching a horror film. Only this wasn't a film. It wasn't a story. It was real, so real that talking about it felt fake. There were no words for it. There was just that night and what happened. Only one other person could ever understand.

"Gage," Amber said. "He—"

"He found you." Mariah was always finishing Amber's sentences for her. "He carried you through the flames. Oh Amboo! I know you were terrified!"

Since there were no words, *terrified* was as good as any. Mariah's eyes were suddenly shiny, and she reached for tissues from Amber's tray table, then smooshed into the chair beside Lottie. When she rested her head on Lottie's shoulder, Lottie rested a cheek on her head. Amber loved looking at them then. Her two besties, her forever-and-ever friends, scooched together into one bundle. If their friendship really was a ship, Lottie would be the trusty rudder and Mariah would be the beautiful figurehead, plowing fearlessly through the waves. Amber would be—who knew what *she'd* be. But she'd be there.

"Oh no!" Mariah jumped up. "I sat on the flowers."

She held up the bouquet, which now resembled roadkill.

"I told you we should've brought her Skittles instead," Lottie said, and then they were laughing, remembering fourth grade, when for science fair they'd microwaved different candies including Skittles to try to prove what, exactly? The deformed Peeps were the best, they agreed. Also, remember that sleepover where they ate so many Jelly Bellys, who could ever look at another one as long as they lived?

"What bizarre little kids we were." Mariah pulled her hair out of its bun and let it waterfall around her shoulders. She smiled. "Remember our old sleepover game? *If your house was on fire and you could only save one thing, what would you pick?*"

Amber blinked. All of a sudden, out of nowhere, she was so angry she could hardly see.

"Nothing!" she cried. "I didn't save a single solitary thing!"

Leaning over the bed rail, Mariah tried to put her arms around Amber. Her hair gave off the scent of that jasmine shampoo they all loved and Amber, who'd only had a sponge bath since being admitted, worried that she smelled bad.

"That was totally insensitive," Mariah said. "I'm sorry!"

"I'm not mad at you," Amber said.

"You're mad at everything," Lottie said. "And who can blame you? Anyway, never mind. The only thing that matters is that you and your family are all right."

"If anything had happened to you, Lot and I would've died." Mariah clapped a hand over her eyes. "I cannot stop saying stupid things. I should just shut up."

"It's okay," Amber said, but really, she was suddenly so tired all she wanted was for them to go. Never, ever had she felt that way about her best friends before.

"It's been too strange this year, being on different teams at school, and soccer takes up so much time." Mariah's eyes were shiny again. "But I'm here for you, Amber. You know that, right?"

"I know, Ri."

"We better let you rest," Lottie said. "But first, on the count of three. One, two, three!"

"Miss you like the tundra misses trees!"

They fussed with her covers, plumped her pillows, then said goodbye, taking the destroyed flowers with them. Kevin came in to replace her IV bag.

"You've got a great posse," he said.

"I know," Amber said.

She'd wanted her friends to leave, yet she already missed

them. Nothing made sense. Everything was confusing. Lottie and Mariah were her besties, yet it felt like they'd visited her from some distant planet.

She lowered the bed, closed her eyes. Mariah's question, a question they'd asked each other before, always in play, just fooling around—why did it hurt so much now?

What one thing would you save?

Promise

The next afternoon Dad brought her a new outfit—unfortunate-looking jeans and a baggy sweater.

Shoes, though. He'd forgotten to buy those.

Kevin gave her a pair of the hospital's dorky shower sandals. "They're at least as cool as Crocs. Maybe you can start a new fad."

The absolute only thing she'd miss about the hospital was Kevin.

Dad signed the discharge papers, and then Amber got back in the wheelchair and they went up to say goodbye to Gage.

A massive bunch of helium balloons bobbed in the corridor outside his room. As they put on their gowns and masks, a nurse carrying a fruit basket half as big as she was joined them. She knocked on Gage's door, and they all went in.

"More treats!" she told Gage, holding up the basket. "Sorry you can't keep them, love. Fruit and flowers can harbor mold or other organisms that cause infection. And our main goal is to keep you free of that, isn't it?" She turned to beam at Amber. "My goodness. Are you the sister?"

"Yes."

"And you must be the proud father." Like a walking sun, she turned to beam at Dad. "We see our share of sadness here. But your family, my goodness. Such valor. Such love!" She held out the giant fruit basket. "Would you like to take this home? We've got flowers at the desk, too."

"You can give it all away," Gage said, his voice gruff. "Give it to other patients."

"You really are a darling, aren't you?" She handed Dad the card attached to the basket. "We'll save all the cards for you." She carried the basket out.

Dad read the message aloud. "'Gage, your extraordinary courage inspires us all. Our community has never been prouder.'" He paused, coughed, cleared his throat. "'Warmest wishes for a speedy recovery. From Cloverville High School PTA.'" He coughed again. "That's very nice."

Gage turned to the window, though there was nothing to see except the roof of the parking garage. Today the burns on his hands looked even more furious, like his skin was trying to curse.

"Little does the PTA know you hate fruit," Amber said.

"People need to quit making such a big deal out of this," her brother said to the window.

Except for the bushy eyebrows, Dad had the kind of face that was mostly straight lines—narrow eyes, arrowhead nose, thin lips. Not exactly a *hard* face, but nobody would call it soft. So now, when it crumpled around the edges, Amber felt like a hand was reaching inside her, giving her heart a squeeze.

"Sorry, bud," he said, "but saving your sister's life is a big deal. Get used to being a hero." He poured Gage a cup of water and set it on the tray table. "I'm taking Amber to Aunt Nor's. You rest. Take your meds, drink your fluids. Nutrition is very important."

Amber could see (one of those things she didn't want to see but couldn't help) that Gage was relieved they were going. She tried not to be hurt. Hadn't she felt the same way about Lottie and Mariah? *He's tired,* she told herself. *He's exhausted and no wonder.* When Dad had described Gage's burn treatment—peeling off his dressing, scrubbing away dead skin, applying antibiotic cream to the wound, putting on a new dressing, doing the whole thing again and again—she could hardly stand to listen.

"What Dad said," she told her brother. "Rest up. We want you out of here and home with us."

As Kevin pushed her toward the elevator, she closed her eyes, stuck her fingers in her ears, and focused her feeble brain waves into a shining beam of light.

Gager, so many words feel useless and stupid now and sorry *is definitely one of them, but I am. So so sorry I went up to your room that night. I'll make it up to you. Not that I ever can, but I promise to try.*

Kevin wheeled her past carts of soiled linen, carts of half-eaten meals, carts of medical supplies. The hospital was all about ugly metal carts. How could Dad work at an urgent care? Spend hour after hour in a place where people were in pain, where bad news could be just around the corner?

They rolled by the visitors' alcove again. A weary-looking woman tried to soothe a fussy toddler, and an old man carefully ate a sandwich. That same girl with the sketchbook was there, only today her head was in her hands.

She must hate the hospital too.

Amber's First Lie

In Dad's car, Amber reached for her phone to tell Lottie and Mariah she'd been discharged, then remembered. No phone. It was like when the electricity went out but you still automatically flicked the light switch as you walked into a room. Your brain knew but your body couldn't remember. She leaned back with a sigh just as Dad spoke.

"I'll be leaving you with Mom, then going to my motel." He said it calmly, like he was describing the weather, not dropping a bombshell.

"Motel? What motel?" Nobody had told her this. "Aunt Nor won't mind if you stay too! She always says the more the merrier!"

"We can't impose on her like that."

It was no secret that Dad and Aunt Nor were not each other's favorite people, but still. Didn't they all need to be together now? What a ridiculous question. Of course they did!

"I've got a suite with a kitchenette," Dad said, as if that made everything all right. "Hey, give me a smile. You've got to be brave, okay?"

She looked down at her shower sandals. She *was* being brave, as brave as she knew how to be. Not as brave as Gage, but that was impossible.

"That's my girl."

They didn't speak again till Dad pulled up in front of Aunt Nor's. She and her family lived in the next town, on a street of expensive-looking homes with perfect lawns. You had to wonder what the neat-freak neighbors thought of her yard, which was a mess of campaign signs, toppled-over bikes and scooters, homemade bedsheet ghosts dangling from the trees. Dad switched off the engine.

"I need to ask you something. Earlier that night, did you go down to the basement?"

"No." And then, remembering, she added, "Gage did though, to get the laundry."

"That's a miracle." Dad grimaced. "I guess I should stop finding fault with your brother."

"I guess!"

"The fire department says the fire started there."

In the basement? The dungeon-y basement? CLEAN OUT BASEMENT was on Dad's long list of work that the house needed, but it hadn't happened. It was still cluttered with junk: a scratched-up love seat, a vintage artificial Christmas tree, old curtains and magazines and who knew what else, all of it left behind by past tenants. Nobody went down to the basement except to do the wash and to retrieve the non-laundry items Clancy tossed down the laundry chute.

"They also say the kitchen smoke detector wasn't working."

Oh no. No no *no*. The battery! If Dad knew Gage had taken it out and not replaced it? Amber stared at the dangling bedsheet ghosts. This was exactly the kind of thing Dad got on Gage's case about—doing stuff halfway, never following through, not trying hard enough. He was so proud of Gage right now, but if he knew why the smoke detector hadn't gone off?

"That's my fault, Dad. The casserole spilled over and the alarm wouldn't stop so I—I took out the battery. I guess I forgot to put it back."

"And your mother never noticed." He frowned.

"I guess not." *Please don't blame* her. Amber dug her nails into her palms, bracing for his anger. A moment ticked by. Another moment.

"I appreciate you telling me the truth," he said then.

The new sweater he'd bought her was suddenly itchy. The car was suddenly too small. The smell of pine air freshener was too strong. Telling Dad a lie twisted your every nerve, and she jumped when he knocked his fist on the steering wheel.

"I should've been there," he said. "This never would've happened."

She believed him. If Dad had been home, the fire never would have started. It wouldn't have dared. Dad would have forbidden it. That made no sense, but Amber believed it. Dad kept the world in order. He kept them safe. When she looked at him now, she knew they both felt the same way. The world had gotten away from them.

"I'll make it right," he promised. "When I get the insurance money, I'll make everything right again."

Aunt Nor's front walk was uneven, and when Amber wobbled in her goofy shower sandals, Dad steadied her with his strong arm.

Not Really Home

The instant you stepped inside Aunt Nor's house, multitudes of people and creatures descended upon you.

First came Bert (real name Brittany). At least Amber guessed it was Bert, since she held Earrings, a large black-and-white rabbit that her identical twin, Ernie (actual name Erin), never touched. Homer, a candidate for world's most ridiculous golden retriever, came running, a stuffed penguin in his jaws. Next came the little twins, Bacon (real name Baker) and Egg (real name Edgar), racing up from the rec room, Clancy at their heels.

Situation Normal at the home of Aunt Nor (real name Noreen) and Uncle Neither (real name Nazeer).

"You're here!" Aunt Nor wrapped Amber in an enormous, slightly sweaty hug. "Welcome, baby girl!"

Nobody would guess she and Mom were sisters. Mom was small and slight, while Aunt Nor occupied space. Dad complained she overdid everything. She couldn't just have a kid—she had to have twins. She couldn't just have one set of twins—she had to have two. She volunteered for so many "causes" (Dad's air quotes) her own house was a disaster area. No wonder Uncle Neither had a consulting job that kept him traveling. Who wouldn't want to get away?

Aunt Nor's smile dimmed as she turned to Dad.

"Hey, Gus. Are you hungry? Pizza should be here in a sec." She cupped her mouth and whispered, "Bert and Ernie have guilted us into becoming vegetarians, but I got a sausage pie just for you."

Dad set Amber's hospital bag down. Clancy pretzeled around his leg and he smoothed her cowlick.

"Thanks, Noreen, but I'm good," he said.

"Don't BS me! You cannot possibly be 'good'" (Aunt Nor's air quotes).

"Guess I'll be the judge of that." This was Dad's idea of a joke, but it sent Aunt Nor's hands flying to her hips. Dad held up his own hands. The battle of the hands!

"Listen, I can't thank you enough for what you're doing."

"Don't insult me, Augustus Price. Our home is yours. No thanking allowed!" Her sleeves flapped like purple wings when she spread her arms. "You do need to explain why you're not staying here. We have plenty of room, especially with Nazeer traveling for work so much these days. Bathrooms would be a little bit of an issue but hey. The family that pees together stays together!"

"You've already got too much on your plate," Dad said.

"I have a very big plate," Aunt Nor said. "It's more like a turkey platter."

Why didn't Mom chime in? Urge him to stay? She wanted him to, didn't she? Instead she hung back, looking lost inside a big sweatshirt that must belong to her sister. Dad un-Velcroed Clancy from his leg.

"Girls, I'm counting on you both to help your aunt and mother. Clancy Chim-panzee, you behave. Lamber, if the cough comes back or you have even the slightest trouble breathing, tell one of us right away, understand?"

With his jaw set so tight and his voice so stern, those could not possibly be tears in his eyes.

But they were. Was she the only one who saw them?

"I utterly refuse to say goodbye." Clancy folded her arms. But Amber hugged Dad hard, and Mom followed him out to his car. The door hadn't even shut behind them before Aunt Nor puffed an exasperated breath.

"That man's part Vulcan." She knocked her fist against her wide forehead. "Don't mind me. I need a filter installed between my brain and my mouth."

"Want to hold Earrings?" Bert handed Amber the rabbit. She and her twin, Ernie, were in fifth grade, not yet middle school, which made them seem almost unbearably innocent.

"He looks like he's crying but that's just because he's so old his tear ducts are blocked."

Cuddling the soft, furry bundle, Amber watched her parents from the living room window. They were talking. Dad was, anyway. Mom just twisted her hands. When the pizza guy pulled up, Dad got into his car and drove away. Mom carried the pizzas back to the house, her eyes on the ground like it was littered with broken glass.

On the dining room table: a wine bottle, a milk carton, plates both clean and dirty, a bicycle pump, a laptop, a pair of shin guards, a hairbrush, a dog chew toy, a stack of flyers, a magnetic chess set, and other unidentifiable rubble. Amber recognized the autumn leaf centerpiece—Aunt Nor happily took any crafts Mom couldn't sell. The table was big, but not big enough to hold so much. It must be defying some laws of physics.

After everyone took a slice of pizza, Aunt Nor tapped her wine glass with a random chess piece.

"A toast," she said. "To Meg, Amber, and Clancy. Welcome home."

"This isn't their home," Ernie said solemnly (she said everything solemnly).

"Wait, is that sausage pizza?" Bert cried. "Yuck! Abomination!"

Homer's yellow snout poked up beside Amber and her slice of pizza disappeared. Then Bacon fell off his chair, which Egg found hilarious. None of this fazed Aunt Nor, who clinked her glass with Mom's.

"To family!"

Amber's new sweater began to itch again. Pushing up her sleeve, she saw the gauze taped over the spot where her IV had been. She was floating between worlds. Before and After. Mom and Dad. Hospital and Home (except Ernie was right, this wasn't really home). She might have floated straight up to the ceiling if Aunt Nor hadn't set another mouthwatering slice of pizza in front of her.

"Eat up, babycakes," she said, and Amber obeyed.

The Main Thing

Amber hoped that when her uncle got back from his business trip he'd be okay with the fact that Aunt Nor had turned his home office into a guest room for her and Mom. On the futon: goose-down pillows, an angel-soft feather bed, and one of those weighted blankets, meant to make you feel safe and secure. On the bedside table: battery candles (no flames, please). On the desk: a mister that puffed calming, lavender-scented clouds.

Amber settled herself on the futon, cradling an ancient laptop that Aunt Nor didn't use anymore. (Aunt Nor was incapable of throwing things away—you never knew what might come in handy.) She and Lottie were messaging, sort of. The laptop apparently had never heard the word *instant*.

Lottie: **guess who asked about u today at school? hint: brown eyes**

Amber (heart doing jumping jacks): **4 real? what did he say????**

Nothing, nothing. Amber tapped the laptop. She jiggled her knees. At last...

Lottie (with an evil grin, Amber was sure): **let me think...**

Amber: **carlotta jackson tell me now!**

Lottie: **something deeply profound, like, is amber ok?**

    Amber leaned back on the world's sweetest, coziest, most wondrous futon. Lucas had noticed she was absent. Not just noticed but acted concerned. The laptop was so antiquated it didn't have real emojis, so she sent Lottie a long string of **x**'s.

Lottie: **btw, her highness wants gage's number**

Amber: **waaaa?**

    Her highness was Lottie's glamorous, could-not-get-enough-of-herself sister, Isla. She and Gage both went to Cloverville High, but as far as Amber knew, Isla had never acknowledged her brother's existence. As Amber waited for the laptop to sputter out a reply, Earrings hopped into the room and she scooped the old bunny up beside her.

Lottie: **she says he is a god and courage should rhyme with gage**

Amber: **for once i agree with her royal high and mighty**

Lottie: **that time he was babysitting us and forgot the soup and it started to smoke and I had to use the fire extinguisher cuz he got so freaked out?**

Amber (stroking Earrings's patchy fur): **I remember**

Lottie: **who knew he was a hero waiting to happen?**

    They texted a little longer, but then Lottie had to get off

to help with her stepbrother, Leon, who was three years old and refused to go to sleep unless she kissed him three times each on his nose and his belly button.

Lottie: **Miss u like...**

Amber: **the tundra misses trees**

Amber switched to a search engine. After she typed in *Price fire,* then waited and waited and waited, she was startled by how many links appeared. When she clicked the first one, up popped a photo of a boy in a basketball jersey, his sandy-blonde hair slicked flat. He was smiling the way little kids do in school photos, like *Please make this torture stop.*

Gage, maybe in fourth grade. She scrolled down.

HIGH SCHOOL BOY RESCUES SISTER FROM FIRE THAT DESTROYED THEIR HOME

Late Monday night, Gage Price, a sophomore at Cloverville High School, came home to find his family's three-story wooden house engulfed in flames. Firefighters had yet to arrive. His mother, Margaret Price, an artist, and sister Nancy had escaped to safety, but his sister Amber remained trapped on the third floor. Neighbors say Gage plunged into the burning building to rescue his sister. Amber Price suffered smoke inhalation. Gage remains hospitalized.

There was a quote from Coach Horton, the junior varsity basketball coach, who never played Gage unless the team was already winning by double digits. "Gage has always been a team player. You can bet he's our team hero now." Mrs. Eddison, who lived across the street, said, "He hugged his mother before he ran into the flames. I am an old lady and I never saw such courage in all my days."

The final paragraph read, "Augustus Price, a physician, was not home at the time. The cause of the fire remains under investigation."

Amber stroked Earrings. Dad was a technician, not a doctor. Gage was years older than that photo. And *Nancy*?

The story had gotten so many things wrong, but not the main thing.

Gage plunged into the burning building to rescue his sister.

Dreams

Bad dreams. That night she had another one. She woke up, heart thudding, unsure where she was. Someone was crying. Something hissed. She lay still, too scared to breathe.

But it wasn't the hiss of fire. It was the lavender mister. And when Amber rolled over on the futon, she saw her mother's hair spread like ribbons across her pillow. Amber wrapped a silky strand around her hand and stroked it with her thumb, like when she was little. Her mother turned toward her.

"Mom. Were you crying?"

"No. I mean, yes."

"I keep crying over every random thing. I can't help it."

"Maybe...maybe we're trying to wash the fire out of us."

"That sounds right," Amber said, snuggling closer. "I wish Dad was here. And Gage. I wish we were all back together."

It was Mom's turn to stroke Amber's hair. "Me too, sweetie."

This was how it was with Mom. Comforting. Cuddlesome. But also, always, a little bit sad. Amber didn't know if anyone else—Dad or Gage or Clancy—noticed this, but she did. Mom had something missing. Or maybe not missing, maybe just tucked too deep inside to get out.

"Bacon keeps farting." Clancy stumbled in, rubbing her eyes. "And Egg sings in his sleep."

She climbed onto the futon. Mom pulled the covers up over them all, and soon Amber fell sound asleep again.

Bro

The next night, Amber borrowed her aunt's phone and called Gage.

"Aunt Nor?" he said.

"No, it's me." In the background, she could hear boys' voices and bursts of laughter. "Are you having a party or something?"

"The team's here. They brought me a ball. A freaking Wilson Evolution and everyone signed it."

A cheer went up. Gage said something that got swallowed up by bro laughter.

"But you're only allowed to have two visitors!"

"The nurses love me so much, they made an exception."

A voice in the background said some cheesy guy-thing about nurses, and more laughter exploded.

"Seriously," Gage said. "No worries, Amberghini. I'm doing great."

But something in his voice was not great. Amber wished she couldn't hear it, because he was a hero and if anybody in the world had the right to feel great, it was him. But his voice sounded flat, like something had run over it.

"If you're tired just tell them to go," she said.

"Gotta book it, little sis!" he said in a fake, dude-ish voice.

"*Little sis?*" she repeated, but he'd already hung up.

She held onto Aunt Nor's phone—it felt so good to hold a phone! Texts were popping up, and even though she knew she shouldn't, she read them. One was for a meeting on the mayoral election campaign, another about a chess club fundraiser. One from Uncle Neither, due back soon from his business trip, made her blush.

When the phone jingled with a call, she was surprised to see *Gus* on the screen.

"Hi, Dad."

"Amber? Didn't expect to get you!"

"I'm borrowing Aunt Nor's phone."

"I know you need a phone."

"I wasn't going to say that, but now that you mention it—"

"I only have a minute. I'm on a break and I need to talk to your mom."

"I'll get her."

Everyone was in the family room, watching *Star Trek*. Mom and Aunt Nor had loved the show when they were kids, or at least Aunt Nor had, and, according to Mom, her big sister had forced her to watch each episode approximately a million times. Now they sat side by side on the sofa, a lumpy beige afghan spread over their knees. As Amber came in, everyone cried that thing about boldly going into the unknown and did the Vulcan salute. Amber did it back, then held out the phone.

"It's Dad."

Mom jumped up and stepped out onto the deck, sliding the glass door closed behind her. Aunt Nor heaved a dramatic sigh.

"So much for living long and prospering." She clicked the remote, ending the episode. Howls ensued, but she said it was bedtime and shooed everyone upstairs. When they'd finally trudged out of the room, she gave Amber the once-over.

"Baby girl, you need some comfort food. How about a bowl of ice cream?"

"I'll get it. You want some too?"

Her aunt's grin said *Is water wet?*

The shelves of Aunt Nor's kitchen were crammed with jars of sauces, boxes of beans and grains. Who knew there were so many kinds of rice? Ditto vinegar? All of her pots and pans shone like new, since if there was one thing Aunt Nor hated to do, it was cook. My kitchen is a shrine to best intentions, she'd say, as she zapped frozen tortillas in the microwave or ordered Thai takeout. Someday, she'd claim, I'm going to use all this wonderful stuff. Just not today.

Amber made a medley of mocha chip, Moose Tracks, and birthday cake. When she carried the bowls back to the family room, hopeful Homer at her heels, Mom was still huddled on the deck with the phone to her ear. Aunt Nor took her bowl and dug in.

"You know what a woman at the food pantry told me today?" she asked.

"What?"

"That the fire was meant to happen. That it's part of a bigger plan we can't understand." Aunt Nor waved her spoon and Homer chased the airborne ice cream. "If I hadn't been holding a sack of potatoes I might've clocked her."

Amber excavated a chocolate chunk. "People say I'm lucky. Am I supposed to feel that way?"

"Do you?"

"No!"

"Listen, baby. People say a lot of things. They think they're helping. But you're the one this happened to." Aunt Nor was a fast eater. She set her bowl on the floor for Homer to lick. "You're the one gets to decide."

"Decide what?"

"What it all means," Aunt Nor said. "What you do with it."

What it all meant? What did that mean? Brain freeze was creeping in. Amber put her bowl down, too, and Homer, overjoyed, began pushing it across the floor with his snout.

"Don't worry about your mom." Aunt Nor glanced toward the deck. "She's made of strong stuff."

Should Amber say that last night she'd woken up to hear Mom crying? She plucked at the afghan, which looked like it had warts.

"I'm her big sister," Aunt Nor went on "I know Meg better than she knows herself."

Gage was her big brother—did he know Amber better than she knew herself? She thought maybe it was the other way 'round. Aunt Nor gently thumbed ice cream from the corner of Amber's mouth.

"I've got plans for your mom. She's always been more talented than she knows, and it's time for her light to shine." Aunt Nor heaved herself off the couch. "But right now, it's suspiciously quiet upstairs. I better see what those hooligans are up to."

A minute later the deck door slid open, letting in a stream of cold air. The look on her mother's face turned Amber's already shivery insides even icier.

"Mom, what? Is Gage okay? He is, right? I just talked to him!"

"Gage is fine." Mom sank onto the couch. "It's our insurance."

Amber exhaled. Insurance! A boring adult thing. But Mom's face was pinched with more than cold.

"To get a mortgage, you have to buy home-owner insurance. We could only afford the cheapest policy the bank would okay. Now it turns out..." She pulled the ugly afghan up to her chin. "It turns out it pays next to nothing toward repairs or rebuilding, and it won't pay anything at all if the fire was caused by negligence or arson."

"'Arson'!" A word they used on detective shows. A *Criminal Minds* word. "Well, we don't have to worry about that."

"There's more," Mom said. "We have to keep paying the mortgage, no matter what. Even if the house is a total loss, we have to keep paying."

Mom looked like she wanted to pull the afghan over her head, the way Clancy hid under her covers when she was scared.

"Mom? Mom, it'll be okay. Right?" Her mother didn't answer, which felt like an answer. Amber's heart dipped. Aunt Nor said it was up to her to decide what this all meant. But absolutely none of this felt up to her.

Meltdown

Gage would be in the hospital a few more days, but Dad said Amber and Clancy needed to go back to school on Monday. He promised it would make them feel more *normal*.

Normal. Another word that had lost its meaning.

Mom's credit card was still in her purse, which was still on a chair in the kitchen, which the fire marshal said was still off-limits, so she borrowed Dad's card to get clothes and supplies from the discount store. The minute they got there, Clancy beelined to the Halloween stuff and pulled a Darth Vader costume, complete with chest armor, mask, utility belt, and signature red lightsaber, off the rack. Mom shook her head.

"We can't afford that, Clance."

"But I need it! I utterly need it."

"Please put it back."

Boom. Clancy was in meltdown mode. She stomped her feet. Emitted a bone-chilling howl. Mom ordered her to stop this minute, which made Clancy go full tilt. For a second, Amber envied her. It would feel so good to just let go! Let it all out! But people were turning to stare. Amber grabbed her little sister's hands.

"How'd you like to be a musk ox for Halloween?"

"For real?" Clancy dug a knuckle into her eye.

"Not for *real*. You want to eat roots and moss? And smell like a wet wool blanket smeared with stinky cheese? You want to weigh six hundred pounds?"

When Clancy started giggling, Mom sighed with relief and mouthed *Thank you*.

On the drive back to Aunt Nor's, Clancy begged Amber to sit in the back with her, then immediately conked out, curling up like a human cashew. Mom caught Amber's eye in the rearview mirror.

"Are you sure you're ready to go back to school?" she asked.

No, Amber wasn't sure. She hadn't missed school at all. Friends, yes, but not the crowded hallways, the slamming lockers, the math pop quizzes, the smelly cafeteria where everyone always sat at the same tables as if hemmed in by electrified fences. Not to mention, now she'd be behind in her work and wearing even-less-great-than-usual clothes. Would everyone feel sorry for her? Or would she be as invisible as ever? Amber didn't know which would be worse.

"Because if you're not..." Mom chewed her lip.

Something in her mother's face—helplessness or hopelessness—made Amber's skin prickle.

"Dad thinks I'm ready!" she snapped. "Why don't you?"

What was she thinking, pitting her parents against each other? Like they didn't do an excellent job of that all by themselves? Suddenly, Clancy woke up with a start.

"My tooth!" She gaped at Amber. The front tooth she'd been wiggling forever was gone. "Where'd it go?"

Mom pulled over as Clancy and Amber unbuckled and searched the back seat. The tooth was nowhere.

"I'm afraid you swallowed it," Mom said. Clancy looked horrified. Amber was sure she'd have another meltdown, but instead her weird little sister cracked up.

"My tooth must be really surprised," she said. "It must be like, 'Where the hell am I now?'"

Mom didn't scold for language. Instead, she started laughing, and then Amber was laughing too. Her body was as surprised as Clancy's tooth.

Who knew it could still belly laugh?

Count on Me

Big as Aunt Nor's house was, the place always seemed to be overflowing. On Sunday night, a campaign meeting took over the living room, Uncle Neither turned the family room into his home office, Mom baked cookies with the (dubious) help of Clancy and the little twins in the kitchen, and the big twins played chess upstairs. Amber retreated to the futon, where she called Gage again. Tonight, he answered right away.

"It's me, the random-phone borrower," she said. "It sounds quiet there. No party tonight?"

"Nah. But some old dude who used to play b-ball for Cloverville came by this afternoon. He runs a chain of shoe stores now and he gave me a voucher for anything I want. I'm praying Dad lets me use it for a pair of LeBrons."

"He will! He's so proud of you."

"I guess you haven't gotten his lecture on charity yet. Did you know the Red Cross called him?"

Red Cross. The words conjured up violent disasters, shocked victims standing next to piles of rubble that used to be their homes. Whenever she saw photos like that, Amber got a pang, then flipped the page or clicked to the next thing. She felt sad for those people, but it was hard to think about them for long.

Those people. Was that her family now?

"'Course he turned them down." Gage made his Dad voice. "We Prices have dignity. We Prices don't need charity."

"I'm not so sure about that. You should see the knockoff high-tops I had to get." She ran a hand over the comforter. "I'm going back to school tomorrow."

"And I'm probably getting discharged Tuesday."

"At last!"

"Except."

She elbowed herself upright. "Except?"

"Dad says I need to rest and Aunt Nor's house isn't good for that."

"What do you mean? You belong here with us!"

"He wants me to stay with him."

"That's bogus! Say you want to come here and he should come too."

"Things are messed up. Mom and Dad can't say two words without arguing."

"I know. But how can they work it out if they stay separated?"

"Don't whine. You sound like a baby."

Amber sank back into the pillows. "I hate that fire," she whispered, sounding exactly like a baby. "Why did it even have to happen?"

He'd never answer such a stupid question and who could blame him. But then he did.

"I keep asking myself the same thing." This time he was quiet so long she thought the conversation was over, but then he said, "Last night Dad told me he wants things to be different between us. He said he realizes he's been too hard on me."

"He actually literally said that?"

"Yeah."

"It was Dad-Dad, not a simulation?"

"I'm trying to be serious with you."

She struggled to think of the last time Dad had admitted he was wrong about something, anything, but she had to give up.

"Amberghini, you gotta help me. This is my chance. Me and Dad? All of a sudden he believes in me, he's even proud of me. I don't want to blow it, but Mom's going to be all kinds of upset if I stay with him. Can you smooth things over? You're so good at that."

Was *that* what she was good at? But her family was in trouble. Something already torn was tearing even more. She didn't want to smooth this over. She wanted to fix it.

Only, how could she refuse to help Gage? How could she refuse him anything, ever again? She closed her eyes, and dragon-tongue flames shot up all around her. She swallowed, tasting smoke.

"Okay," she said. "Count on me."

"I always do."

She loved him so much then.

Amber's Amber

After they dropped Clancy off at her elementary school, Mom drove Amber to the corner where she, Mariah, and Lottie always met to walk the last block to school together. Her friends were already there and they both started waving so hard, you'd think it was a waving contest. When Amber leaned over to tell her mother goodbye, she was suddenly aware of Mom's messy ponytail and hand-me-down sweatshirt, which made her look homeless, which they were, but not really. Mom looked exactly like someone the Red Cross would help.

"Don't worry, Mrs. Price," Mariah called from the sidewalk. Wrangling adults was one of her specialties. "I'll take care of her today!"

"Me too, Mrs. Price," Lottie chimed in.

When Amber got out of the car, her mother eased it forward, braked, backed up, rolled down her window.

"I love you, Amber. Be safe."

"Bye, Mom!"

"Your poor mother," Mariah said as they watched her

drive away. "She must be severely traumatized. She's scared to let you out of her sight."

"She doesn't look very good," Lottie said.

"That's actually kind of mean," Mariah said.

"How about me?" Amber said. "Do I look normal?"

There was an awkward pause when the look on both their faces said *Not really.* Then Mariah laughed, green eyes sparking.

"Never fear. You are about to look *spectacular.*" She handed Amber a mesh jewelry pouch. "Amber, meet amber!"

Amber drew out a delicate gold chain with a honey-colored stone. "Oh, Ri! It's too...too..."

"Too perfect, right? I just couldn't stand the thought of you losing *everything* and having *nothing.* Then my mother said, 'Amber has the chance to start over and make a new beginning. That can be a good thing!' She and I decided you should mark today with something specially meant for you. Lift your hair." She fastened the necklace, then spun Amber back around. "Aww! No fair making me teary. My mascara's not waterproof!" Mariah turned to Lottie. "It's perfect on her, isn't it, Lot?"

"Yes." Lottie swallowed. "It really is."

Mariah was rich. Not rich rich, but definitely richer than either Amber or Lottie. For birthdays and holidays, her gifts were always the most expensive, and Amber secretly looked forward to them more than to Lottie's. Their no-reason gifts to each other were stuff like sparkly pens or Wint-O-Green Lifesavers, never anything like this.

"See that little speck?" Mariah pointed. "It's an insect that got trapped in tree resin a gazillion years ago, give or take. Little did it know, someday it would hang around your neck."

Down the street, the school's first bell rang.

"Uh-oh!" Mariah tossed Lottie a knowing look, then grabbed Amber's hand. "No way we can be late *today*."

It was one of those perfectly beautiful days that come in the middle of October. Golden leaves, a brilliant sky, someone's white cat cleaning its paw beside a pot of red geraniums. Amber's cheap new clothes felt stiff, and Aunt Nor's house had been so topsy-turvy this morning she couldn't get into a bathroom in time to do her hair, but still. Here I am, she thought. Me and my two best friends, hustling to make the bell, just like *before*.

And there was the school, kids crowding the steps to get inside, just like always. Suddenly, going back didn't seem so bad. Like Dad said, things would be *normal*. ELA with her favorite teacher, unbearable math, lunch with Lottie in their private spot by the recycling bins. Life had gone on this whole time without her, as if nothing had ever happened.

The late bell rang as they took the steps two at a time. Just before Mariah tugged open the door, a strange grin lit her face.

"Ready?" she asked.

"For what?"

Mariah flung open the door. "Here she comes!" she yelled.

Ship of Friends

WELCOME BACK AMBER PRICE!!!!!

The banner stretched wall to wall. Every inch was covered with signatures, as if the whole school, all three grades, had signed it. Kids crowded around, doing finger snaps, making finger hearts.

"Yay, Amber! Woot, Amber! Hooray, Amber Price!"

Smiling faces pressed in on all sides. Amber tried to smile back, but she was having trouble catching her breath. Hugs and fist bumps, faces and voices blurring. For a second, Lucas swam into focus, but the crowd swallowed him up.

"Are you surprised?" Mariah asked, then whispered in her ear, "Close your mouth!"

Amber's face scrunched up in a way that she was sure looked totally weird.

"Good people!" The assistant principal, Mr. Monaghan, materialized out of nowhere, his superpower. "Are we forgetting what the last bell means?"

"We're welcoming Amber back," Mariah said, slinging a protective arm around her shoulder. "Her first day since the tragedy."

"I understand, Mariah." Mr. Monaghan straightened his tie. He had a thing for Looney Tunes ties, which almost made you feel sorry for him. Today: Daffy Duck. He turned to the gathered kids. "Cougars! Thank you for this awesome display of empathy for Amber. But we are a learning community, and the mighty bell has rung. To home base now! I want you there five minutes ago."

Groans and moans, but eventually everyone scattered so that only Amber, Mariah, and Lottie were left. Mr. Monaghan smiled at them.

"Girls, it's time to get to class," he said. "Unless Amber needs something?"

"Erm. A new math book?"

"Of course." He gave Daffy a tug. "I meant more along the lines of, do you want to see the school counselor? Do you need to talk?"

The few times Amber had spied the school's one and only counselor, the woman had been rushing down the hall clutching an extra-large coffee and looking frantic. It was hard to think how she could help Amber. It felt more like Amber should be helping her.

"I promised her mother I'd take care of her." Mariah's arm tightened around Amber.

"I promised, too." Lottie stepped up on Amber's other side.

Mariah the figurehead, Lottie the rudder—Amber's own friend-ship! She was about to dissolve into a pool of gratitude when the school secretary leaned out the office doorway.

"Mr. Monaghan? You have a concerned parent on the line."

"One minute!" He turned back to the three of them. "So, who's on Amber's team? Mariah? And uh...?" He gave Lottie a dubious look.

"Lottie." No one did the death glare like her. "My name is Lottie Jackson and I am on Amber's team."

"Excellent." Mr. Monaghan nodded. "Lottie, you look after Amber today. And Amber? Remember, the counselor is here if you need her. As am I. Now come get late passes." He headed toward the office.

"Take good care of her," Mariah told Lottie.

"You don't need to tell me that," Lottie told Mariah.

Which felt really awkward and strange. But what didn't right now?

A Brand-New Book

By the time they got their late passes, home base was over and kids were flooding the seventh-grade hallways. Amber's name was like a song everyone was singing.

"Hey, Amber! Amber, you're back! Yay Amber! We missed you, Amber!"

They had precisely five minutes between classes, so the song ended almost as quickly as it began. Still dazed, she stared into her locker. Which books had gotten burned up? Which ones were still here? At last Lottie grabbed a few things, unzipped Amber's backpack, stuffed them in, rezipped the backpack, closed the locker, spun the combination, and turned to Amber with an anxious look.

"I wanted to warn you about the banner, but Mariah swore me to secrecy," she said. "She said you'd love the surprise, but I wasn't so sure."

"I do." Amber didn't want to sound ungrateful. "It's just I never. I mean. I didn't expect—" Expect people to care? That sounded so pathetic.

When Amber and Lottie walked into ELA, people started clapping. Some of the boys grabbed the opportunity to stomp their feet and hoot like deranged owls. The teacher, Mrs. Oluonye, hushed them, but not really.

"Amber, as you can tell, we're very glad to see you again."

Mrs. Oluonye was Amber's home base teacher, her ELA teacher, and also possibly the kindest teacher to ever walk the face of the earth. In her classroom, desks were in a circle, which meant nobody felt left out but also, nobody could hide.

A pause. Amber realized everyone was waiting for her to say something.

"Erm?"

The class laughed, but in a nice way.

"I mean, thank you," she said. "The banner is so cool." The sun spilled through the window, catching her necklace and making it sparkle. "I'm really happy to be back and I never said that about school before in my life."

This time when people laughed, a rush of pleasure made her a little lightheaded.

"What was it like?" This was Tyler Boswell, the boy Lottie crushed on for unfathomable reasons. "Did stuff melt, like in *Last Inferno*?"

Now everybody started talking.

"Once my grandma was cooking and the grease popped and—"

"Like, kill me now, fire is my worst nightmare! If it was me—"

"Is your brother really getting a medal from the mayor?"

"I heard the governor."

"Friends!" Mrs. O. interrupted. "First of all, what do we know about raising hands? Second and more important, let's give Amber her space. It's natural to be concerned and curious, but she's been through a difficult experience. Amber, it's completely up to you whether and when you choose to talk about it."

All eyes were on Amber. Kelly B. was studying her with an interest she'd never shown before. And Amber didn't have to turn her head to know Lucas was looking at her. She could feel his gaze, warm as the sun spilling through the window. Empty-brained, dry-mouthed, she slid into her seat.

"Sorry," she managed to say. "Maybe another time?"

Maxwell Driver, future felon, blew a raspberry. Everyone was probably hoping to waste the entire class talking about fires, and Amber had let them down. She glanced across at Lottie, who crooked her little finger, their secret sign for *Got your back*.

"Eyes on me," Mrs. Oluonye said in her brisk, cheerful voice. "Back to our study of fables."

Amber tried to focus on how fables were tales with

morals, like *Slow and steady wins the race* or *A weakness may prove to be a strength*. Mrs. Oluonye showed them slides from a picture book, *The Lion and the Mouse*. Amber remembered the story: The lion catches a mouse but decides to let it go, and later, when the lion falls into a trap, the mouse returns the favor by chewing the ropes and setting him free. The moral: *No kindness is ever wasted.*

"Do you think that's true?" their teacher asked. "Does everyone deserve kindness?"

"Not my brother." Maxwell smirked. He was the kind of kid who didn't really belong to any group and acted as if he liked it that way. He was known for wearing the same two football team shirts, both too small, over and over. "My brother deserves a kick in the butt."

"Maybe you want to think more about that, Maxwell," Mrs Oluonye said. "Journals out, friends. Let's free write about kindness for five minutes."

Amber pulled out one of her new notebooks. Opening it, she urged her brain to cooperate. Or at least operate. *Kindness*, she thought. *Lions. Mice. Traps.*

"Having trouble getting started?" Mrs. Oluonye stood beside Amber's desk. For a teacher—for anyone, really—she had the most beautiful wardrobe, dresses and dashikis from her trips to Nigeria and Ghana. Mrs. O. was old and sometimes, like now, she leaned on a cane.

"Beginnings are intimidating," she said, and the only word to describe her smile was *kindly*. "I always have trouble starting a brand-new notebook."

When the five minutes were up, Amber had written exactly one word.

Kindness.

From now till the end of the school year, whenever she opened the notebook, it would be the first word she'd see.

The Price of Kindness

In math, Mr. Getty (aka The Yeti) excused Amber from the pop quiz.

In PE, Mrs. Hoysradt let her rotate out of the volleyball line after a single humiliating attempt to serve.

On the way to lunch with Lottie, a sixth grader handed her a note covered with stickers that said things like WAY TO GO and YOU ARE SPECIAL TODAY. Even two eighth graders noticed her, not that they actually spoke *to* her.

"That's her." One girl nudged the other.

"Which one?"

"The short one."

Two kids wearing *Spread Kindness Like Confetti* T-shirts waited outside the cafeteria. Selena, a seventh grader on Mariah's team, had shiny dark hair and wide gray eyes, but being pretty wasn't what she was about. She was president of the Confetti Club, a club that did school and community projects. Amber had thought about joining, but like so many things she'd thought about doing, this somehow never happened.

Selena was with a short, fidgety boy who, the second he saw Amber, blurted out, "We really want to help! Wait till you hear our supe-dupe idea!"

"Hi, Amber. Hi, Lottie." Selena put a steadying hand on the boy's head. "This is Justin Cotton. He's one of our most enthusiastic sixth graders. On behalf of the club, we first want to say how sorry we are for your loss."

"Nobody died," Lottie said, then looked embarrassed. Amber knew Lottie admired Selena. "I mean, Iggy the Hamster. But no humans."

"It could be our best project ever!" Justin cried.

"I'm sorry," Amber said. "I'm kind of confused?"

"As soon as the club heard about the fire, we knew we wanted to help," Selena said. "We brainstormed and landed on this crowdfunding website called Helping Hearts. It's specifically for people going through difficult times—illness or loss or natural disaster. We'd like to set up a donation link for your family."

"We'll call the project the Price of Kindness!" Justin burst out. "That was my idea!"

"We'd make it a school-wide project. We'd recommend that kids don't ask their parents for money. They'd raise it themselves, by doing things like babysitting or raking leaves or having a bake sale. That way, it would be more meaningful." Selena paused. "Mrs. Oluonye, our adviser, likes the idea. But she said we need your permission first."

The club had discussed her family? They wanted to do a school-wide project?

"That sounds so nice." Lottie gave Amber a little nudge. "Don't you think, Amboo?"

"Sure! I mean yes. I mean..." The smell of cafeteria food was making Amber a little queasy. But it wasn't only that. She was hearing her father's stern voice. *We don't need charity. Not the Price family!*

Selena touched Amber's arm. "I know it's a lot," she said.

"It's a really thoughtful, really generous idea." Amber gazed down at her knockoff high-tops. How could she say no? How could she say yes? "I have to ask my parents."

"For sure!" Selena gave her a quick hug. "Let us know soon, okay? Thanks, Amber. Bye, Lottie."

"Wow. Selena." Lottie shook her head. "*She* thanked *you*."

Miss Luna, the lunch lady who normally scolded them for banging their trays even when they didn't, saluted Amber with her serving spoon.

"I remember your skinny-minny brother! I always gave him extra mashed potatoes. Now look what he did! Goes to show, never judge a dog by its bark!" She set extra chocolate puddings on Amber's tray. "Tell him Miss Luna says get well soon and God bless."

Two seconds after the day's last bell, Mariah was at Amber's locker. Her cheeks were rosy, her eyes green as clover. A walking summer day, that was Mariah.

"I'm ditching soccer practice. You're coming to my house. We'll wallow on my bed and eat junk. Savannah will be so glad to see you." Savannah was Mariah's adorable pet parrot.

"Ahem." Lottie cleared her throat and Mariah did an eye roll.

"All three of us, of course," she said, and adjusted the necklace she'd given Amber. "Hey, isn't Selena amazing? The Price of Kindness—it's so genius."

"Ri!" Amber was startled. "You already know about that?"

Mariah grinned. "Am I your best friend or am I your best friend?"

On the way out, they stopped to study the WELCOME banner. Amber found Lottie's square, precise printing, Mariah's loopy cursive. A name was scrawled in the middle of the *R* of AMBER, too high to make out. Mariah went up on her toes and squinted.

"'Wish I could get with you, from Lucas,'" she pretended to read.

"Shut up!" Laughing and blushing, Amber swung open the front door, nearly clipping her math teacher Mr. Getty, who stood just outside. "I'm so sorry!" she yelped. "Excuse me!"

When he saw Amber, his famous Yeti scowl morphed into an approximation of a smile.

"No problem, Ms. Price."

Mom was parked across the street. Leaning out the car window, she called, "Amber! I'm in a hurry!"

"Tell her you and Lottie are coming to my house and staying for dinner," Mariah commanded. "My mom will drive you home."

But when Amber asked permission, Mom shook her head.

"The fire marshal is meeting Dad and me at the house, and I promised Aunt Nor you'd babysit for her this afternoon. Get in! Your father will pitch a fit if I'm late."

"I just have to tell Mariah."

Who stuck out her lower lip. "Snap."

"I know." Everyone was trying to be so nice, yet she'd been letting people down all day. "Sorry."

Mariah tossed her hair. "Guess I'll go to soccer practice after all."

"Sorry," Amber repeated.

"Text us!" Mariah called after her.

Amber would have reminded her that she didn't have a phone, but soccer girls had begun clustering around her. Climbing into the back seat next to Clancy, Amber saw Lottie linger on the edge of the group, swing her viola case a couple of times, then turn and walk away alone.

Walk in My Shoes

The second Amber got out of Mom's car, Aunt Nor rattled off her babysitting instructions: The big twins were at after-school chess club and she'd pick them up on her way home. The little twins had to practice their spelling words before they even thought about video games. Homer had eaten a box of crayons so there could be intestinal issues...

"...and some nice church lady dropped off a box of clothes for you kids." Aunt Nor was digging in her bag, approximately the size of a sofa pillow. "Where the fudge are my—here!" Keys in hand, she kissed Amber on the forehead and hustled to the garage.

A large, sealed-up cardboard box sat in the hallway. When Amber opened it, she found a note on top: *For the Price children. Yours in hope and faith, Fairview Presbyterian.*

The clothes on top were Clancy-sized, and the next layer must be for her. Amber lifted out sweaters and T-shirts, a flowered dress that definitely should be repurposed as a tablecloth, a pair of leggings. Next came things she could tell would be too big for her skinny brother. All the clothes smelled fresh and clean. Basically, they were as good as anything she and her friends might have found at the thrift shop, with one major difference. She hadn't chosen them.

At the bottom of the box was a pair of girls' boots. Their soles were scuffed, but they looked more expensive than any shoes Amber had ever owned. They made her think of a book she'd once read about a girl who'd traveled across the country trying to find her mother. Amber had loved the story, which was full of twists and turns and made her cry at the end. The moral was something like, *You can never truly know someone else till you've walked in their shoes.*

Amber zipped and unzipped one of the boots. Had the girl who'd owned them worn them to school? To church? To parties with friends? Had she been loud or quiet, funny or serious, popular or invisible? Even if Amber put the boots on and walked for miles, she'd never know what that other girl was like.

As nice as everybody had been to her today, why did she feel so lonely?

Amber carefully refolded the clothes, set the boots on top, closed the box, and pushed it into the hallway closet. She found Bacon and Egg in the basement rec room playing a video game while Clancy beat them over the heads with a Nerf bat, demanding they give her a turn. On the rug sat two gift baskets. The one holding cheese, crackers, and other healthy-looking items was untouched. The one with sweets had been ransacked. Amber read the attached cards.

For the Price Family from your friends at Nature's Best. Eat healthy, be strong!

For the Prices with comforting wishes from Sweet Surrender.

"It says 'Price,'" Clancy complained, tossing aside her Nerf bat. "These dudes are hogging up our candy."

"You're living in our house," Bacon replied. The younger twins were easier to tell apart: Egg's nose was pointy while Bacon's turned up at the end. "That means you have to share with us."

"I do not!" Clancy said. "Do I, Amber?"

"It would be nice of you," Amber said.

"But I don't have to!"

"Did you guys practice your spelling words?" Amber asked. Deafening silence. She tried again. "Look at this delicious fruit basket. How about we take it outside and have a picnic."

"We hate playing outside." Egg's eyes didn't budge from the screen. "We like to rot our brains."

Amber sank into a beanbag chair and pulled her little sister into her lap.

"How was your day? Did you make utterly perfect choices?"

"Maybe." Clancy twirled her cowlick, then touched Amber's necklace.

"Do you like it? Mariah gave it to me. It's real amber. See the little bug inside?"

"He's dead?"

"Well, yeah."

"I hate dead stuff." Clancy's face scrunched up. "Iggy's dead."

Maybe Bacon was losing, or possibly his heart held a hidden, tender spot for his cousin, because he offered Clancy his controller.

"Your turn," he said.

Back upstairs, Amber emptied and refilled the dishwasher. She put away a bag of groceries (More rice? Pink salt?). She perched on a stool at the island and read campaign literature. Aunt Nor's candidate for mayor, Shontel Bibb, was trailing in the polls, and her coma-inducing flyers could not be helping. Homer scratched at the back door and Amber took him into the yard, where he pooped out a waxy rainbow.

Late-afternoon clouds were scudding in, and as she hunched her shoulders against the chill, she tried to picture her parents at the house. Amber hadn't seen it since the night of the fire and now she began to remember random things, like the flowery dining room wallpaper she thought was pretty but Mom planned to tear off, and the old-fashioned pantry Clancy called the panty. Amber curled her toes inside her knockoff high-tops as a wave of homesickness broke over her.

Not just homesickness for home. For the whole entire *before*.

Where was Mom? Shouldn't she be back by now? Maybe she and Dad were talking things over. Maybe they were realizing what Amber already knew. Disasters were supposed to bring families together, not push them apart.

Homer started barking, and she spun around. Mom's car was coming up the driveway.

Tentacles

Her mother hauled two garbage bags inside and set them on the kitchen floor. A faint smell of smoke wafted out and Amber pinched her nose. The fire had no right to follow them here!

"The smoke got into everything." When Mom pushed her hair back from her face, her fingers left a faint dark trail. "And the soot! The marshal told us it can contain cyanide and I forget what else. Not to mention the danger of toxic mold from all the water." She squeezed her eyes shut, like she was trying to unsee it all.

"Mom?"

"Sorry!" Her mother's eyes flew open. "It was just such a shock, so much bigger than I expected. But wait. Wait. I have one nice surprise." She pulled something out of the cloth bag she'd been using as a purse.

"Is that really my phone?" Amber grabbed it and pressed the home button. It stayed dark, but still. Her phone had survived! Like a long-lost pet, it had found its way back to her. This was a good sign, right? She pointed at the garbage bags. "What's in there?"

"Not much, I'm afraid. Just what the firemen managed to retrieve. They wouldn't let us go upstairs due to 'structural instability'—that's what they call it. The damage is so bad, they still can't pinpoint the exact cause." Mom turned to the sink and carefully washed her hands, then dried them slowly, one finger at a time. "You can guess how angry that makes Dad. I've never seen him so furious."

Dad always wanted to understand the *why* of a thing. Of every single thing. Even his job as a radiology technician was about looking deeper, hunting for reasons people were sick.

Mom suddenly pressed the dish towel to her eyes. "Why didn't I put the battery back in the alarm? Why wasn't I paying attention? Where was my head?"

"Mom! It's not your fault!"

"If the alarm had gone off and we'd known sooner, maybe..." Her mother clutched the dish towel. "I'm sorry, sweetie. I should be asking you about school. How was your day?"

The banner, the cheers, the fundraiser, Lucas and Selena and Mariah and Lottie. Amber got that feeling again. Like she lived on a different planet from her friends.

"It was okay. But did you and Dad talk about—I mean, Mom? What do we do now?"

Mom folded the dish towel, set it down, and began

opening Aunt Nor's cupboards, pulling out cans and boxes. Homer came skidding into the kitchen, hoping for something to eat.

"Gage is getting discharged tomorrow." Mom set a like-new skillet on the stove. "Dad's found an apartment." For a second, Amber's heart lifted, but her mother went on quickly, "For him and Gage. It's one-bedroom so it will be a little tight, but they'll manage."

Amber gripped her dead phone. A separate apartment? That was way more serious, more permanent, than a motel.

"Dad knows how to manage Gage's dressings and his other outpatient care." Mom began to chop an onion with quick, sure flicks of her wrist. Unlike her sister, she was a wonderful cook. Amber watched her open a can of tomatoes, then carefully run her finger around the rim. She always did this, checking for bits of metal that might get in their food. "And the apartment's much closer to the old neighborhood, so when he's ready it'll be easier for him to get to school and his job at Convenient Mart."

Amber sank onto a stool. She'd promised Gage to smooth things over with Mom. But Mom didn't seem upset. She kept her back to Amber as she went on talking.

"It's better if we're not together right now. Dad keeps looking for something or someone to blame. I said what difference does it make, what good does blaming ever do, and he said... Well, never mind what he said. I'm sorry, sweetie. Your dad and I aren't good for each other right now."

Amber watched her mother add fake meat and herbs to the pan, then stir with a wooden spoon. When at last she turned around, her eyes were red. Mom always looked slightly frazzled, but now? *Exhausted* was the word.

"The one bright spot is, he's so proud of Gage. That's the only thing giving him any joy right now." Mom put her wrist to her forehead. "I could really use a hug."

But when Amber put her arms around her mother: smoke. Amber stiffened, and Mom stepped back.

"I know—I need a shower. Keep an eye on the sauce, okay?"

When her mother left the kitchen, Amber opened the garbage bags. What had the firefighters salvaged? A pair of flats she'd saved up forever to buy but then, as soon as she got them, they were over. A porcelain angel (one wing missing) that Clancy had given Mom for Mother's Day, then taken back to play with. A framed certificate naming Dad employee of the month. An unopened sack of hamster food.

Amber kicked a bag. The fire didn't care what it ate! Trash or treasure, it was all the same. The fire didn't stop to ask *How much did this laptop cost? Whose heart will break if I destroy this sweet diorama or fry this helpless little hamster?* Like the worst monster in the worst nightmare, there was no reasoning with fire. Until something stopped it, it kept right on grabbing things with its yellow-blue tentacles and stuffing them into its hot, greedy mouth.

Amber twisted the tops of the bags closed. Almost too late she remembered the sauce and stirred it before it burned. Now the boy twins and Clancy were stampeding up from the rec room, and the girl twins and Aunt Nor were piling in the back door, and everyone was saying how delicious it smelled and how hungry they were. Here was Mom, freshly showered, starting water for the pasta, and Aunt Nor doing what she called the Spaghetti Dance, and then they were all sitting down together with heaped plates except for Ernie, who had her perfectly plain pasta in the same cereal bowl she used for every meal. Then Uncle Neither got home from his downtown meeting and squeezed in at the table, where Homer was making his rounds, setting his hopeful snout on one knee after another.

It was nothing like orderly, mannerly Price family meals. This family was a rushing river, forever on the verge of flooding.

Amber fingered her new necklace. The fire had eaten their things. Their old life was covered in soot. As she slid the pendant on its chain—the honey-colored stone, the tiny life caught inside—it was like she was sliding back and forth, back and forth, not knowing where she'd come to rest.

Jessie

That night, as Amber waited for a turn in the kids' bathroom, Ernie (Amber could tell it was Ernie by the solemn expression) handed her an old phone charger.

"Mom never throws anything away," she said. "This one should work."

Amber fetched her phone, attached the charger, and plugged it in. Together, they watched as the screen lit and the tiny lightning bolt appeared.

"Ernie! You saved my life!"

"Actually," Ernie solemnly replied, "that would be your brother."

Selena and Justin were waiting outside when Amber, Lottie, and Mariah got to school the next day.

The fundraiser! Amber had almost forgotten about it and then, when she remembered, she'd been afraid to bring it up with either of her parents. What if Mom said yes and Dad said no? The last thing Amber wanted was to give them another reason to argue.

"So?" Justin practically levitated with excitement. "Did your parents give the okey-dokey?"

Lottie crooked her pinkie in their *here for you* signal, Mariah made big-eyes, Selena smiled a patient smile. How could she let them down?

"It's so nice of you," she said. "I mean, what can I say besides thank you?"

She only meant to stall, but they took it for a yes. Mariah hugged Amber, and then she hugged Selena, too. Justin, wearing a hopeful expression, maneuvered into place for his own hug, but Mariah ignored him.

"How can I help?" she asked Selena. "I really want to be involved."

"Me too," Lottie said.

"Don't worry." Selena's smile was ear to ear. "This is going to be a major school-wide effort."

During math, Amber was called to the office, where the secretary gave her the rolled-up welcome-back banner and a Snickers bar. She was wondering what to do with the banner when the bell rang, doors flew open, and the stampede began. Lucas miraculously emerged from the herd.

"Need help?"

"I'm not sure what to do with this. I don't want to just smoosh it up in my locker."

"I'll run it to the music room." He took it from her. "Mr. Halliday won't mind. You can get it at the end of the day."

His eyelashes were so thick, they made shadows on his cheeks.

"Thanks," she said. Such a brilliant remark!

Lucas smiled. He smiled at everyone—it didn't mean anything. Amber's brain knew that, but her heart had its own ideas.

Just before lunch, she ducked into a stall in the one girls' bathroom where you could always get reception. Their school had a no-phones rule, probably made up by the same committee that decided to name their teams for birds of prey, but Amber really wanted to talk to Gage. He was coming home today, not that *home* was the right word. Probably she shouldn't bother him. She should wait till he settled in and had a chance to rest. But her phone was already in her hand and her fingers were already typing.

Got my phone back obviously!!!

She was waiting for a reply, reading the gray metal walls of the stall and wondering who *JT + LR* were, when someone else came in. Peeking under the stall door, she saw a pair of Birkenstocks. When she stepped out, a tall blond girl spun around, phone clutched to her chest.

"Hi, Jessie," Amber said.

Jessie Morris was new this year. She was a Falcon, like Amber, and once or twice Amber had helped her find her way through the rat-maze hallways. But Jessie was a loner. One of those kids who, back in elementary school, would have sat on the Buddy Bench because they had no buddy to play with. Now she gave Amber a tiny smile. A fraction of a smile.

"Hi, Amber." Her phone buzzed and she quickly turned away. "Mama," she said, then dropped her voice so low all Amber heard was "I can't."

Jessie was the kind of person you knew you should be nice to, but it was hard to be around her for long. Her sadness or shyness or whatever it was made you feel too helpless. Also, to be completely honest, you worried that whatever *it* was might be contagious. Today, though, Amber found herself lingering in the bathroom, washing her hands, peering in the mirror, checking her phone again, trying to think of something nice to say to Jessie. But Jessie kept her back turned, and at last, Amber gave up and went to the cafeteria.

She grabbed a tray (today Miss Luna added two extra chocolate puddings and a slice of coconut cake) and joined Lottie at their table, ringside to the blue recycling bins.

"Where were you?" Lottie asked.

"Texting Gage. He's getting out of the hospital today." She surreptitiously checked her phone again—going to a phone-free school was inhumane—and was happy to find a message.

with dad more soon

She quickly texted back **k**, then slid the phone into her backpack before she got caught. An empty pop can sailed through the air and into the bin behind them.

"Three points!" Maxwell pumped his fist like he'd actually done something notable.

Lottie, who adored fries but thought grease was bad for her skin, started blotting them with a napkin. Not the most appetizing thing to watch.

"Ready for something hilarious?" she said. "Isla wants to ask Gage out. I told her you and I are like sisters and if she tries to date Gage, it will be some kind of very bizarre incest. She told me she was horrified by my depraved and perverted mind but please still get his number." Lottie stabbed a grease-less fry with her spork. "Actually, she didn't say depraved or perverted, her vocabulary is much too primal."

Amber peeled the top off a pudding cup and finger-scooped some pudding. From their corner spot, she had a view of the whole room, but she didn't see Jessie. Come to think of it, she'd never seen Jessie here. Where did she eat lunch?

Outside the window, some kids were kicking a soccer ball around the playing field, while others clustered in little groups beneath the trees. Lottie was still talking about Isla, and Amber was still thinking of Jessie, and now an old memory floated up. Lottie and Isla's mother had died of some aggressive kind of cancer. It had happened very quickly, or at least that was how Amber remembered it. When Lottie came back to school afterward, she'd hide behind the playground willow tree so nobody would see her crying. Nobody except Amber. More than anything, Amber had wanted to help, but how? What could she do? What should she say? Watching her friend cry like that was so terrible and scary, Amber just wished she would stop.

One day, as Lottie huddled behind the willow, Amber stamped her foot and told her to quit being a crybaby or else. Lottie stared at her, then ran off, leaving Amber alone beneath the tree's drooping branches.

Now, as she watched Lottie opening ketchup packets, she realized her best friend had been only slightly older than Clancy when her mother died. How horrible Amber had been to order Lottie to stop crying! Bad things—a mother dying, a terrible fire—they could happen to anyone. Why hadn't she ever understood that before?

Did bad things have to happen to you—you *personally*—before you could understand?

That didn't seem right. It seemed like a failure of humanness. But maybe it was true.

"Amboo?" Lottie stopped dousing her fries and tilted her head. "Why are you looking at me like I'm an ice cream cone you dropped on the sidewalk?"

Before Amber could answer, Melissa Thom strode up to their table. Melissa belonged to the smart-but-not-nerdy group. An eighth grader and the editor in chief of the school paper, she wore blouses and dark red lipstick, as if prepared to step before a news camera at any moment. Amber tried to nonchalantly wipe her pudding-coated finger on a napkin.

"Hi, Amber. I guess you know you're the top story around here." Melissa flashed a professional smile. "The paper's coming up on deadline for one of our two print issues, and I'd love to feature you. I have a meeting after school today, so we'll have to do it tomorrow. How about early, before home base? Is that okay with you? Or is there a better time?"

"Erm..."

"Terrific. Meet me in the library. I look forward to talking." She gave Amber's sticky hand a firm shake and strode away.

Improvising

In the music room, recorded jazz was softly playing, or at least Amber, who knew nothing about music except the kind she listened to, guessed it was jazz. Mr. Halliday, the band and orchestra teacher, nodded at her from his desk. In the back of the room, Lucas was running a cloth over the push-downy things on his trumpet. When she said hello, instead of answering he blew a line of round, sweet notes.

Who knew a trumpet could sound dreamy?

"That's so pretty," she said, and Lucas laughed. Unlike most people who laughed a lot, he didn't sound nervous or silly. He simply sounded happy.

"Just improvising," he said.

"That means making it up?"

"Sort of. It's like inventing and collaborating combined." He showed her a laptop with a program for recording notes. "Mr. Halliday lets me come in here after school and mess around."

"He does more than mess around," Mr. Halliday said without looking up.

"I take chorus. I could never play an instrument." She

lowered her voice so Mr. Halliday didn't take offense. "I wouldn't have the discipline to practice."

"It's not discipline if you love it," Lucas said.

"Mariah's that way with soccer. It's like her religion."

"Yeah, I guess." He didn't seem that interested in Mariah or soccer. His black curls tumbled over his brow and she tried not to stare at how cute that was but it was possible she did and now her cheeks were heating up. "So, not sports, not music," he went on. "What are you into?"

All of a sudden, Amber's awkwardness disappeared. Poof! Lucas was asking her a real question. He actually wanted to hear her answer.

"I wish I had something," she said. "I feel like I'm still trying to figure it out."

For once, he didn't smile. Instead, he nodded as if this made perfect sense. The banner was in the corner and as he gave it to her, their hands touched.

"You will, I can tell. Hey, welcome back, Amber."

Amoeba Part 2

"Dad keeps the heat so freaking low," Gage said when she talked to him that night. "It's like we're stationed in an Arctic outpost."

"How do you feel? I mean, besides freezing your bum off?"

"Okay. It's just that one burn. The docs say it's healing great but it looks like a piece of rotten meat. That a dog chewed on. Then puked up. Dad says it's a badge of honor." Gage snorted. "He keeps saying stuff like that."

"It's true though."

"They're easing me off the pain meds. There goes my chance to become a junkie."

"That's really not funny."

"You know what's really not funny? Pizza Corner offered us six months of free pies and he said no thanks."

"Noooooo! Pizza Corner is the best in the universe!"

"Prices don't accept charity." The Dad Voice. "'How many times do I have to tell you that?'"

"Speaking of Dad? It's possible I'm in trouble." Amber slid her pendant side to side. But before she could say more, he told her to hang on, he had to take another call.

She waited, knees drawn up, inhaling lavender mist, till Gage finally came back.

"Who was that? Never mind, I know you won't tell me." She waited a moment, just in case he might, then said, "Here's my problem. This club at school wants to do a fundraiser for us." She started to describe the Price of Kindness, but her brother cut her off.

"No way," he said. "Tell them no way."

"I tried."

"You tried? What do you mean?"

"I mean..." *I mean, I'm an amoeba!* "I didn't know how to say no. And besides, what's wrong with it?"

"It'd be too weird. You want the whole town pitying us?"

"You're channeling Dad."

"Seriously, Amber. Tell the other kids thanks but no thanks. Get them to shut it down."

"But why? People are only trying to be kind." Melissa, Selena. And what about Lucas? He'd just finally noticed her! Amber hugged her knees. "They want to help us, Gage. They'll be so disappointed if I tell them no."

"Well, then, they'll be disappointed."

"I don't get why you—"

"Amburger." He made a funny gulping sound, then added, "I'm beat, gotta go. Sorry."

"You don't ever have to be sorry." She bit her lip. "Not ever."

He said goodbye, but his words echoed in her ears. Why was Gage being so stubborn? He was shy, that was one thing. But the bigger thing was, he knew Dad wouldn't want the fundraiser. Gage didn't want to make Dad angry, and who could blame him?

Amber slid her pendant back and forth on its chain. *You can make a new beginning,* Mariah said when she gave it to her. Things were new, that was for sure. But were they beginning or ending? Lottie said time was circular, not linear, but Lottie was always saying things too profound or mathematical for Amber to comprehend.

Back and forth, back and forth.

Whose Story?

Melissa was waiting in the library when Amber got there. Mr. Barrow, the librarian, wearing his usual uniform of chucks and an old concert tee, was watering his plants, and an earthy scent wafted over the room. Amber sat across from Melissa, who'd set out a yellow legal pad, several pens, and her phone.

"Mind if I record?" Melissa tapped the phone.

"Okay." Like she was in a film, playing the role of star witness—that was how it felt. She watched Melissa print *Amber Price* at the top of her yellow pad.

"We all know the facts of what happened." Melissa sat perfectly erect. How did you even get posture like that? "What our readers really want is *your* story. If you could describe the experience in your own words?"

Amber cleared her throat. She tried to sit up straighter.

"Well," she said. "It was just a normal night. Except I fell asleep up on the third floor, in my brother's room. When I woke up, I realized the house was on fire. I knew I had to get out, but I didn't know how."

"What was the fire like?" Melissa asked. "Could you give more specific details?"

"I mean, there was a lot of smoke. Thick, stinky smoke." Amber hesitated. "And it was hot."

"Hot?"

"Like, extremely hot." Amber slumped in her chair. Melissa clicked her pen a few times and Amber tried again. "And noisy. I never knew fire could be so noisy." Her brain was fuzzing over. It didn't want to go back to that night. It refused to supply words to describe *the experience.*

Melissa leaned forward. "You must have been very scared."

"Duh!" Amber blurted. "Sorry! I don't mean to be rude but scared doesn't cover it. I was afraid I was going to, you know."

"Die?" Melissa, human yardstick, asked. When Amber nodded, she made a note. "Amber, can you talk about your brother? What's he like?"

"My sister and I have always looked up to him. I mean, we *literally* look up to him, because he's taller than us, even though he's short, all of us Prices are, but I also mean we look up to him..." Her brain fuzzed out.

"Figuratively?" Melissa offered.

"That's it." By now Amber was too warm. She pulled

out her water bottle and took a gulp. "He loves basketball, he eats his own weight every day, he has an extensive collection of hoodies. Or he did." Another slug of water. Melissa slid her phone closer, as if to make sure it recorded what came next.

"Your brother walked through fire for you," she said. "Were you surprised by his courage?"

Amber lowered her eyes. How could she answer with a yes or a no? Gage had never *acted* brave before, but he must have been. A person couldn't suddenly, out of nowhere, do what he had done. His courage must have been folded inside him, like an acorn waiting to become a mighty oak.

But that was a complicated answer, and she could tell Melissa was hoping for something more dramatic. Melissa wanted to write a great story.

Only this wasn't Melissa's story. It was Amber's. Amber's and Gage's. Something Aunt Nor had said came back to her. *You're the one who gets to decide what it all means.*

Amber took another drink of water. Now she needed to pee. She set down the water bottle.

"Gage is quiet. People don't notice him much." For a second she felt like she was describing herself. "But as his sister I can say he's capable of anything he sets his mind to. My parents have always been super proud of him." That wasn't true, but it should have been. A trickle of sweat ran down between her shoulder blades. "Everyone is calling him a hero now, but guess what? He's always been a hero to us."

She watched Melissa write down *a hero to us* and underline it twice.

"Perfect! Amber, I have just one more question. Your family lost pretty much everything in the fire. Can you describe how that feels?"

Pen poised, Melissa pursed her ruby-red lips. Really, for such a smart person, how could Melissa even ask? It felt terrible. It was a nightmare! But instead of saying the obvious, Amber said what she hoped, what she wished with every bit of her slumping, sweating self, was the truth.

"My family lost everything," she said. "But we still have each other, and we always will."

Dung Load

When she came out of the library, Selena and Mariah pounced on her.

"Justin set up the link," Selena said. "Our goal is—"

"Seven thousand dollars!" Mariah said. "By the first week in November."

"We're ready to announce it, but—"

"We wanted to tell you first!" Mariah covered her mouth. "Sorry to interrupt! I'm just so amped." She and Selena fist-bumped.

"Seven thousand dollars?" Amber drew a breath. She was still sweaty from the interview and by now she really, really needed to pee. "That's so much money."

And I don't know how to say this, but you have to call the whole thing off immediately.

"Here's a secret," Selena said. "We set a goal we're sure we can reach. We expect to get even more. Justin will make the announcement this afternoon." She smiled like a fond mama. "The boy is dying to do it!"

"Isn't it so incredible?" Mariah gave Amber a squeeze before rushing off to her home base.

By now kids were pouring in for the day, some in groups, some alone, some laughing, some looking like they were on their way to a jail cell. Amber beelined to the restroom and was on her way to her locker when Kelly B. stopped her. Kelly was a dancer, and she wore her blond hair in a sleek, never messy bun. Her eyebrows were perfectly plucked, and now she arched the left one.

"Mariah told me about the fundraiser," she said. "Just so you know? My friends and I are all in."

"Really?" *My friends* was a synonym for the *ultra-popular-no-matter-how-hard-you-try-you-will-never-be-one-of-us group*. "I mean, thanks, Kelly."

"One hundred fifty percent."

"Thanks!"

Amber dove for her locker and spun her combination. What was she supposed to do now? Gage had begged-ordered her to shut down the fundraiser. Plus, Dad? He wouldn't even take free pizza. What would he say to seven thousand dollars?

Making Dad angry was Gage's department, not Amber's. But now her father and brother would both be angry, not to say furious, with her. She tried the combination again, but the lock refused to open.

"What a morning, we all overslept, then Leon started throwing up, my dad was already at work so Rasheeda had to drive me even though she's having wicked Braxton-Hicks contractions, I don't smell like vomit do I?" Lottie was suddenly standing beside her, out of breath, spinning her own locker combination. She glanced over at Amber. "May I ask what you are doing?"

"Someone must've changed my combination overnight. I can't get it open."

"Are you okay?" Lottie twirled the dial and yanked Amber's locker open. "You look like Leon. You're not going to puke, are you?"

The day somehow went by, and now it was last period and afternoon announcements. Justin's eager voice came over the PA.

"This is Justin Cotton with a special announcement from the Confetti Club. Our motto is 'Spread kindness like confetti!'"

Amber slid down in her seat.

"Our club believes that even if you can't help everyone, everyone can help someone. As you know, our classmate Amber Price and her family recently suffered a tragic fire. Her brother, Gage, a former student here at Cloverville Middle, performed the heroic act of saving her life. However, sadly, the Price family lost most of their possessions. To get them back on their feet, the Confetti Club is announcing a fundraiser." Justin paused dramatically. The mascot for the whole school, all the grades and all the teams, was a cougar. He went on, "Cloverville Cougars, please go to the website Helping Hearts dot org, where you will find our project, the Price of Kindness!"

Amber kept her eyes on her desktop. Maybe Gage and Dad were right after all. This felt weird and humiliating.

"You can donate online or give money directly to our adviser, Mrs. Oluonye," Justin was saying. "Please do not pester your parents for money. Earn the bucks yourself. Every little bit will help. And remember this. How do we change the world? One act of kindness at a time!"

Somebody clapped. There were finger snaps. Looking up, Amber discovered people smiling at her.

"This is great," someone said.

"I'm so in," someone else said.

"Me too."

"Me three."

The merciful bell rang and Amber quickly gathered her stuff. But when she started for the door, Maxwell was in her way.

"Seven thousand dollars." He gave a shrill whistle. "That is a dung load of money."

"Speaking of dung loads, please move." Lottie stepped up beside Amber.

"Mind your own business, crater face." But Maxwell turned and shuffled away.

"It *is* a lot of money," Amber said.

"Correct!" Lottie bugged her eyes.

The end-of-the-day hallways buzzed even louder than usual. The Price of Kindness had caught people's interest. Justin, in the center of a knot of kids, pointed as she passed, and everyone turned to wave. Kelly B. detached herself from her followers to give Amber a one-arm hug. Tyler, Lottie's misguided crush, was suddenly in front of them, walking backward.

"Guess I'll be spending my weekend raking leaves to earn money," he said. "Thanks so big, Amber Price."

"Watch where you're going, gooney bird!" Lottie said.

"Takes one to know one, Blottie." The approximate response of a second grader, but Lottie blushed as if he'd recited a love sonnet.

Lottie went to the restroom and Amber went to her locker, which she once again couldn't open. She was tilt-a-whirl dizzy. Who'd have guessed people would get so excited about the fundraiser? A fundraiser for *her*? Till now, middle school had basically been all about knowing where you belonged. You had your true friends. You had the lunch table where you were welcome, and the teacher who liked you even though you were far from her best student. Those were your stepping stones across the treacherous river that was middle school.

But what if she'd gotten it all wrong? What if school wasn't just about who was who and where you belonged? What if everybody had kindness tucked inside them, just waiting for a chance to show itself? The same way Gage's hidden courage had come bursting out of him?

Mrs. O. was in the hallway. Her poster with the words *Beauty is truth, truth beauty* was coming loose from the wall and she was struggling to fix it.

"I can help!" Amber held the poster while Mrs. Oluonye sticky-tacked it back.

"Thank you, Amber!" She stepped back and smiled. "The fundraiser seems off to a good start. I hope it's not too overwhelming for you."

"It is, a little." Amber's voice came out a squeak, and Mrs. Oluonye looked concerned. Another person Amber would disappoint if she had to end the project. "But it's so nice and I'm—I'm really grateful."

"Promise you'll come see me if a little overwhelming turns into a lot?"

"Okay."

Amber returned to her stubborn locker.

She had to convince Dad and Gage! Either that or quit school.

Historic Sleepover

Mom was famous for how slowly she drove. We'd make better time riding a glacier, Gage always complained. Amber usually didn't mind, but tonight, after the strangest week in the history of her life, she couldn't wait to get to Mariah's house. They were having a sleepover, the first one since summer, and she leaned forward, trying to make the car speed up. Mom stopped at a corner.

"Dad wants you and Clancy to come for dinner Sunday," she said.

"What about you?"

"He didn't invite me." Mom kept her eyes on the traffic, letting every car within five miles go by. "He's happy about one thing, though. The insurance company decided to do their own investigation." She finally made the turn. "Insurance people don't fool around. If anyone can find out how the fire started, they will."

Mariah's mother hugged Amber, then hugged Mom. While the two mothers talked in the entryway, Amber ran upstairs to Mariah's room. Lottie was already there.

"Three friends!" cried Savannah, Mariah's African gray parrot. Savannah was beautiful, all silvery feathers with a ruffle of snow-white around her eyes and a bright red tail. (She was also smarter than some people Amber knew.) "Three friends!" she repeated, sidling back and forth on her perch. "Three cheers!"

Amber had been in this room who-knew-how-many times, but tonight she looked around in wonder. Mariah had always owned more of everything than she did. Before, that was just how things were. Now, the muchness of Mariah's life was a little startling.

"You judging my mess?" Mariah pouted.

Amber smiled. Did Mariah even *know* how much stuff she owned? "You have the world's best mess."

"Best mess!" Savannah chortled. "Best mess!"

Mariah had laid in supplies of their favorite snacks and drinks, and when her father came home with sushi, he'd even remembered the seaweed salad Amber loved.

It was just like before.

"Can I ask something that will sound strange?" Amber petted Savannah's neck. "Could we please not talk about you-know-what? Could we pretend it's ye olden days, before everything?"

"Backward time machine—I love it!" Lottie said.

Amber ate sushi till she was a walking California roll.

Sprawled on Mariah's thick carpet, she listened to Lottie talk about how The Yeti was trying to recruit her for Mathletes. Of course she loved math, but did she want to spend her extremely limited free time drilling with the team, not to mention her weekends at competitions?

"Not to mention," Mariah said without looking up from her phone, "being labeled a nerd."

Lottie stiffened. "Nerd is an offensive term."

"I agree, but you know how dumb people can be." Mariah set her phone down. "On the other hand, the Mathletes have a tradition of being more male than female, so you have an obligation to represent."

Lottie looked at Amber. "What do you think?"

"It's up to you, Lot." Amber smiled. "Number people are your people! For me, imagining being a Mathlete is like...I might as well imagine being an opera singer."

"An opera singer? What is that supposed to mean?"

"Just...unimaginable."

"It sounds like you agree joining the team would officially make me a dork."

"I didn't say dork!" Mariah cried. "I said nerd and I agreed it was dumb."

Lottie looked so miserable, Amber walked her fingers across the soft, creamy carpet to tap her knee.

"Don't stress, Lot. You'll figure it out."

"Exactly," Mariah said. "All right, come on. Selfie time."

"No way!" Lottie crooked her arm over her face. "I'm getting my period and my skin is a combat zone."

"You never want to be in photos!"

Lottie believed she looked worse in photos than in real life. Which was totally untrue, because Lottie was pretty whether in 2D or 3. Just try to convince her, though.

"You always have an excuse," Mariah said. "If you really don't like the way you look, you ought to do something about it."

Lottie froze. If Mariah saw how hurt Lottie looked, she pretended not to.

"Come on! Just one picture," she begged. "Please? Hashtag Price of Kindness."

Lottie shook her head. "We promised Amber not to talk about—"

"I know, but people are already doing it."

"Doing what?" Amber asked.

"Posting! How they plan to earn money. Memes like *Change the world one kindness at a time*. It's becoming a thing."

"A thing!" Savannah squawked. "A thing!"

"Please?" Mariah clasped her hands. "This is about you, Amber. We're practically required to post! Just one photo and I promise you get to choose which one, Lot."

They took a bunch. Cheesing with Savannah, squished

together in the saucer chair, toasting with their drinks. Once they got going, they even made a couple of videos. After she'd posted one of them doing jazz hands, (Lottie's choice since her face was covered), Mariah pulled up YouTube and they tried to learn the steps to a new dance, but by then they were so full of ginger beer and flavored seltzer they kept burping, which made Savannah say, "Pardon me, madam!"

They'd collapsed on the bed in hilarious exhaustion or maybe exhausted hilarity when the door opened and Mariah's mother came in.

"Mama! You know you're supposed to knock!"

"I'm sorry, but this is an emergency. Lottie, your big sister just called. Rasheeda has gone into labor."

Lottie bolted up from the bed. "The baby's not due for six weeks!"

"She and your father are at the hospital. Isla said she called but you didn't pick up."

Lottie grabbed her phone. "Three missed calls." She started to call back, but Mariah's mother put a hand on her shoulder.

"I said we'd drive you home. Mariah, help Lottie gather her things. Dad's getting the car out."

Lottie grabbed her backpack and sleeping bag and rushed out the door.

"Bye-bye," Susannah said.

"Mama?" Mariah leaned into her mother, who wrapped her in a hug. "What's going to happen? Will the baby be okay?"

"I'm sure everything will be fine. Babies are born much earlier than this." Her brow furrowed, though, and she touched the tips of her hair, which was the same beautiful auburn as Mariah's, only cut in a crisp bob. "I guess it's just you two tonight," she said.

"You two!" Savannah agreed. "You two!"

"Let me know as soon as you hear from Lottie." Mariah's mother gently closed the door behind her.

"This is terrible," Mariah said. "What if the baby dies?"

"Mariah! Don't even!"

"Why not?" Mariah threw herself down on her bed. "It could happen. Since what happened to you, I keep thinking how everything can turn awful just like that. In a heartbeat." She put her hands over her eyes. "I know I promised not to talk about it, Amboo, but I can't help it. Some nights lately I can't sleep. I think about huge stuff like pandemics and earthquakes and wars and endangered species, and also stuff like school shootings and cancer, and the world feels so, so dangerous. Like it's out to get us."

Was Mariah just being dramatic? It didn't seem like it.

"We're made out of glass and we don't even know it."

Mariah's voice was small. When Amber lay down beside her, she whispered, "I don't want to."

"Want to what?"

"You know." Mariah let her hands fall. "Die."

One of the many wonders of Mariah's room was the ceiling, which was painted pale blue with wisps of white clouds. You could pretend you were outside on a summer day, gazing up at the sky. The two of them did that together, side by side, Mariah sniffling and Amber stroking her arm.

"Let's not ever die," Mariah whispered.

"Okay."

"Promise?"

"Swear!"

"Swear!" Savannah crowed.

In the morning, they found the group text Lottie had sent around 4:00 a.m.

New bro James is here tiny but ok

They tried to call but she didn't pick up, so they sent happy texts, then filmed themselves doing a dance of jubilation and sent that too. They ate the super-delicious pastries Mariah's dad bought from the fancy bakery.

"This was epic," Mariah said as Amber packed her things. "Historic." She folded her arms. "I want to say something but it might sound mean, so I won't."

"Yes you will."

"I'm glad we had time alone just the two of us. There. I said it." Mairah turned away to straighten her many bed pillows. "You know I love Lottie. But you're different when she's not around."

"What? No I'm—"

"Yes you are! When it's just the two of us, you're... looser."

"Did you just call me a loser?"

"Very funny." Mariah made a face. "I'm not trying to badmouth her. I'm talking about *you*."

"Okay."

"You need to think about yourself more, Amboo. You've been through a trauma. You should only do things that make you happy." Mariah crossed the room and opened her closet. It was the kind with double rows of hangers and built-in drawers. She gave it a game-show-hostess wave. "Pick out some stuff. We're different sizes but lots of things will still fit."

"What are you even talking about?"

"Look at all these clothes. It's ridiculous."

"You already gave me a necklace!"

"You can return the clothes once you get the Price of Kindness money." Mariah started throwing things on the bed. Her style was different from Amber's, partly because she could afford the best brands but also because Mariah never minded people looking at her. She held up a turquoise top with sparkly buttons. "This would look perfect with your hair."

"You are cuckoo," Amber said, grinning.

"One other thing I couldn't say when Lottie was here? Kelly B. wants to invite you to her Halloween party."

"I repeat. Cuckoo, cuckoo."

"Cuckoo, cuckoo!" Savannah said.

"I know we always thought Kelly was super annoying, and she kind of is, but people are complicated. Since I've been on the Eagles team, I've been eating lunch with some of her friends. We've hung out a few times on the weekends."

"You never told me that."

"I know but anyway. Kelly can actually be nice when she wants to. She's sick of dance because she has to worry about gaining weight, which is so wrong, but her mother won't let her quit. And her father has anger issues. Her life isn't as perfect as you think." Mariah lifted her shoulders and let them fall. "Anyway, she really does want to invite you."

Amber sank onto the bed. Kelly B.! She and her friends had the kind of parties that Amber only heard about. Having viewed several zillion online photos, she had a clear idea of how amazing those parties were, but she, Lottie, and Mariah never dreamed of getting invited.

Except now, apparently, Mariah did.

"Did you get me invited?" Amber asked. "You did, didn't you?"

"It's probably the other way around. She invited me because I'm your best friend." Mariah kept pulling clothes out of the closet and tossing them on the bed.

"Is she inviting Lottie too?"

"How should I know?"

But the look on her face said she did know.

"She's inviting Lucas," she said. "Just FYI."

Amber pretended to faint, and Mariah buried her in a pillow avalanche.

Late that afternoon, Lottie and Amber finally talked. Everything was okay, Lottie said. Actually, everything was total chaos, since there'd been some complications and baby James needed to remain hospitalized in something called the NICU and Rasheeda was exhausted from the difficult delivery, and her father had had a minor car accident because he was such a nervous mess, and in the midst of everything Leon had gone missing and Isla had called the police, who found him asleep behind the couch, but considering how terrible things might have turned out, everything was okay. For now.

"We're basically operating like people living on the side

of an active volcano. Anything could happen any moment." She heaved a sigh. "What'd you two do after I left?"

"Nothing. Just fooled around." Amber pushed the thought of what Mariah had said about her being different without Lottie into a corner of her mind. "We made a pact to be immortal."

"That's highly inconsiderate. If people lived forever, there'd be no room on the planet for anyone new to be born."

"We were only playing, Lottie."

"I know." She sighed again. "I guess I just don't feel like joking right now."

"I get that."

And then, in stereo, "Miss you like the tundra misses trees!"

It was only after they hung up that Amber wondered, Did a tundra actually miss trees? Wasn't a tundra *supposed* to be tree-less?

Helpless

Dad's new apartment was like an army barracks. Not that Amber had ever seen an army barracks, but she guessed that this was how they looked. Spare. Orderly. Charmless. Dad had bought an ugly brown couch at the thrift shop and the price tag still dangled off an arm. On a rickety end table stood the lamp Aunt Nor had given them one Christmas. The fabric shade was gone but the base, made of metal and shaped like a golden retriever, had survived the fire. Amber had always loved that goofy lamp, but tonight, in this apartment, it looked like a relic from some lost civilization.

Dad poured cider and they sat sipping, polite as if they were at a formal tea party.

"This is awkward," Clancy said.

Gage wore a new hoodie, sleeves pulled down over his burns. He'd gained a little weight and even looked taller, though probably that was just his new LeBrons.

"What is that?" Clancy pointed at the casserole Dad had set down. Behind his back, Gage gripped his throat and did the silent scream.

"A nurse at work brought it in for me." Dad poked it, looking doubtful himself.

"I'm a vegetarian now," Clancy said. "Does this contain animal products?"

Gage's phone began to buzz and he stood up. "Sorry. I gotta take this."

Amber gaped as he went into the bedroom and shut the door behind him. In the Price household, you had to grovel on bended knees to take a call during a family meal, and even then, the answer would be no.

"He's allowed?" Clancy was just as surprised.

Dad, Master of Rules, gave a helpless shrug.

Wait. Helpless? Dad?

"He gets calls and texts all the time," Dad said.

"He's popular," Clancy said. "Like me. I'm extremely popular now."

"Do you even know what 'popular' means?" Amber asked.

"It means like a wizard. You have powers. Can we send out for pizza?"

"You have good food in front of you," Dad said.

"How come Gage can talk on the phone but I can't have pizza?"

"Those two things are not connected."

"You like him better now! That's how come he stays with you and not us."

"Clancy, just eat." Dad turned to Amber. "How about you? Have you caught up at school?"

Amber pushed an unidentifiable lump around her plate. Usually, when Dad asked about school, all she had to do was tell him that she'd watched a film about mitosis, or that she'd miraculously sunk a foul shot in PE, and he'd be satisfied.

Tonight she had something big to tell him. Something enormous. Eyes on the grayish lump (meat? potato? dryer lint?) she lost her nerve.

"Math is still hard," she said.

One good thing about Dad. He never checked their online grades. He said that was their responsibility.

"Keep trying," he said, followed up by a Certified Dad Saying. "The things that come hardest are the most rewarding."

The things that came hardest? Okay. Amber tried again.

"There's—at school? Some kids want to do a fundraiser for us."

Dad's bristly eyebrows lifted. "Say more."

"It's a club. The Confetti Club? Kids do projects for good causes." She fixed her eyes on her gross-out plate. Now he'd say their family wasn't a cause. Now he'd say—

"Go on."

"The fundraiser is called the Price of Kindness. I mean, it would be called that. If they actually did it." Amber set down her fork. "They're really excited to help us, Dad."

"That's very nice, Amber. But we're doing fine."

"This couch is giving me an allergy." Clancy pushed away her untouched plate. "At recess Eva said there's no such thing as hamster heaven. She said when you're dead you're dead and that's it, end of story."

All the straight lines in Dad's face softened. "Should we get you a new hamster?"

"No! I want Iggy back!"

"Clancy," Amber said. "You know that can't happen."

"I tried to save him but Mom dragged me away!" Clancy looked outraged. "We left him to die!"

"Mom was saving *you*," Dad said.

"What if he thought I didn't love him anymore?"

"Who?" Gage came out of the bedroom. "Who thinks you don't love him? Not me!" He swooped Clancy off the couch and swung her around, making her squeal.

"Careful!" Dad said. "Watch your arm, Gage!"

But Gage swung her again, the two of them spinning and hooting, Dad shaking his head as he covered the casserole.

"Uppie!" Clancy did her baby-talk voice. "More uppie!" She gripped her big brother's arm and Amber saw the pain shoot across his face. He lost his footing and something tumbled out of his hoodie pocket. He scooped it right up, but not before Amber saw what it was. When he set Clancy down, she lurched dizzily into the coffee table, knocking over the dog lamp and sending cups of cider sideways.

"For the love of Mike!" Dad said.

"Hang on. I got this." Gage hurried into the kitchen and Amber followed. As he grabbed some paper towels, they heard Clancy begin to cry.

"I want to go home," she said. "Our real home."

"Clancy-dancy," Dad said.

"I don't like Aunt Nor."

"None of that now! You should be grateful to your aunt."

"She called you an a-hole. Mom told her hush but I heard her."

Amber's and Gage's eyes locked. He pulled his hoodie over his mouth, smothering a chuckle.

"It's not funny!" Amber said, but laughter bubbled up inside her, too.

"Aunt Nor's got a big mouth." Gage wadded the paper towels. Amber caught his sleeve.

"Why do you have a lighter in your pocket?" she whispered. "I know you're not smoking."

"Me? After what my lungs went through? What kind of nut job do you think I am?"

"I don't know." She smiled, though she felt uneasy. "How many kinds of nut job are there?"

He spun away toward the sink and turned on the water. When he pushed up the sleeve of his hoodie, she saw his arm. Bandages still covered the worst burn, but she could see the smaller ones, the blisters collapsed and yellow, the skin around them sickly pink. All her anger vanished.

"The lighter belongs to a friend," he said, voice low. He wet the paper towels under the faucet.

"What friend?"

"What are you two doing in there?" Dad called. "Hurry up!"

"I'll tell you, I promise." Gage turned the faucet off. "Just not now." He hurried into the living room. "Here, Dad," he said. "Let me clean that up."

Back and Forth

Clancy suffered another minor meltdown when she had to say goodbye to Gage, but she soon fell asleep in the back seat of Dad's car. It took Amber a while to realize Dad wasn't going straight back to Aunt Nor's. Instead, he was detouring through their old neighborhood. The Convenient Mart where Gage worked, Koko's Bakery where she always got the mango tea, Revolve Thrift where she and Lottie loved to hunt for treasures. One after another, the old places slid by the car windows. When Dad passed the library and turned left, her heart began to beat faster.

Moments later, he stopped in front of their old house.

Oh.

Oh.

Boards covered the lower windows, and the front door was crisscrossed with yellow caution tape. Broken glass, charred wood. A black streak shot up to the third floor, where the narrow attic window gaped blank and empty.

The smell of smoke—the house still exhaled it. It seeped into the car, defeating Dad's pine tree air freshener. Though

Clancy was sound asleep, Amber threw her arm across her little sister's shoulders to protect her.

"Your mother said seeing it might—what do they call it? Trigger something. But I thought you should see."

Amber did not want to see. She did not. But Dad trusted her to handle this, and she wanted to live up to that. He thought she was stronger than she really was, and she hated to let him down. Still, when they drove away, she buried her face against Clancy's shoulder.

"It's bad," Dad said. They stopped at a red light and he beat the palm of his hand on the steering wheel. "From what they tell us, it's not worth trying to save the place."

Amber lifted her eyes to look at the back of her father's head. He needed a haircut. Dad never needed a haircut. He always went to the barber before his hair had a chance to get the tiniest bit messy. The light turned green and he drove on, not speaking again till they were almost to Aunt Nor's.

"What did you say the kids wanted to call their fundraiser?"

Startled, she said, "The Price of Kindness."

"Kindness. I approve of that."

Was kindness different from charity?

When the car stopped in front of Aunt Nor's, Clancy woke up. Her thunderstorm mood had evaporated and she kissed Dad, then scrambled out and ran up the front walk.

For someone who supposedly hated Aunt Nor's house, she was in a big hurry to get inside. Amber was about to follow when Dad turned around to face her.

"We don't need other people's help. I might not have made that clear to you." His furry eyebrows knitted together. "But the way people are reacting to what Gage did, that's something else. I don't want to disrespect that. A day doesn't go by that we don't hear from one of his old teachers, coaches, whatever. Everyone's so proud of him, but it feels like more than that. It's like he proved something important about *them*, too. Like he's reminded us all that everybody's capable of big things." He ran his hand up over the back of his head. "Gage hates the attention, but he deserves it. He deserves every last bit of it."

Aunt Nor's front door opened and Homer bounded out, jaw bulging with tennis balls. (He could carry three at once—his special talent.) Mom stood in the doorway.

"Homer!" she called. "Homer, come back here!"

But what Amber heard was *Home! Home! Come back here!*

The house's light bent around Mom, giving her a golden halo. Dad ran a hand up the back of his head again, making his hair stand on end.

"You better help catch that dumb beast," he said. He looked at Mom a moment longer, then restarted the car. "Maybe next time your mother will come for dinner, too."

"She said she wasn't invited."

"Is that what she told you?"

"I don't know. I think so." *Don't put me in the middle!* "Anyway, I'll tell her, Dad."

Just before bed, she got a group text from Kelly B., inviting her to the Halloween party. Amber could see all the names on the list, a Who's Who of seventh grade, plus some other kids who didn't fit any exact label. Kids like her. And Lucas.

Not Lottie, though.

Amber slid her amber pendant back and forth, back and forth.

Dad was against the fundraiser.

But the fundraiser was happening.

Dad wanted Mom to come for dinner.

But Mom didn't want to go.

Amber was invited to The Party.

But Lottie wasn't.

People kept calling Gage a hero.

But he kept wishing they wouldn't.

Back and forth.

Good and bad.

Before and after.

Back and forth.

More Questions

On Monday, Amber wore the turquoise top Mariah had given her. She fastened all the sparkly buttons, but as soon as Mariah saw her, she undid the top two.

"You want to look like a total priss?" She settled the pendant against Amber's bare skin. "There."

Lottie was going to be absent for this week. Baby James was still in the hospital and her parents were traveling back and forth all day. Lottie had to fill in, helping with the house and Leon. Isla was supposedly helping too, but she had such an important life, with so many important obligations, and she was in high school where it was a disaster to miss even one day and blah-blah-blah.

As Amber stood by her locker, trying to organize her backpack for the day, she realized how much she relied on Lottie. It took planning to decide which supplies you needed for the first half of which day and which you could leave in your locker to avoid being crushed by a ten-ton backpack, and usually she just did whatever Lottie did.

Of course Amber forgot her math book. Like Dad, Mr. Getty didn't tolerate excuses. Rules! Rules made things possible. Incredibly important things, such as understanding the difference between the associative and commutative property of addition. If you forgot your book in Mr. Getty's class, you were doomed to spend the entire humiliating period trying to peer at someone else's.

But today, miraculously, Mr. Getty set a spare book on her desk. He did it without a word, strolling past her to the front of the room where, on the whiteboard, all those a's, b's and c's danced in and out of parentheses. She opened the book and was desperately trying to follow the lesson when a note traveled across the room and onto her desk. Amber unfolded a drawing of a huge snow creature, face twisted in agony as it began to melt. At its enormous hairy feet, hands on her hips, stood a girl wearing a sparkling necklace.

You thawed The Yeti.

Amber looked up. Lucas touched two fingers to his brow and saluted.

Her heart flapped like a bird trapped inside a house. Carefully, so carefully, she refolded the note and slid it into her backpack. Who knew math class could be a place of joy?

But when the bell rang, Mr. Getty called her to his desk. His beard was snowy white, his eyes icy blue.

"How are things, Ms. Price?"

"I'm sorry I'm behind. I know I need to work harder."

"I meant..." His beard quivered. "Personally."

Was it possible? The Yeti was attempting warmth?

"I'm okay," she said.

"I'm glad to hear that." He pursed his thin lips. "I understand things might be erratic for you right now. It might be hard to concentrate on your studies. You could find math rewarding at a time like this. Math is dependable. There's nothing like math for certitude."

"I'll try," she said.

"I'm here to help. By the way, I hope the fundraiser is a big success."

Amber thanked him, then escaped into the hallway, where she plowed directly into Lucas.

"'There's nothing like math for certitude,'" he intoned, catching her arm.

"Don't make fun!" she said. "He can't help being a walking icicle."

"I'm not making fun. I believe in certitude. And attitude and latitude and étude and all the tudes. I'm a tude dude."

As they walked down the hall side by side, that wonderful Lucas-calm descended upon her.

"You know what's funny?" she said. "I think Mr. Getty actually believes binomial equations can save the world."

"Give the man credit. He believes in his mission. It's like Mrs. O. with literature and grammar and all. They keep on preaching, even though most kids couldn't care less." He smiled. "Teachers—they got them some fort-i-tude."

She smiled back. "Are you saying they deserve our grat-i-tude?"

He walked her all the way to her locker, and then, as he walked away with his bouncy, springy step, he called back, "I'm not big on math either, but if you ever want to study together, say the word."

She told herself that Lucas was all about equal-opportunity niceness, and that just because he'd sent her a note, and waited for her outside class, and walked her to her locker, and offered to help her with math, it didn't mean anything.

It was just Lucas-i-tude.

Amber was walking to her locker before lunch when Kelly B. fell in step beside her. Kelly's dancer legs were so long and muscle-y, Amber had to scurry to keep up.

"You're coming to my party, right?" Kelly B. said. "If you can't afford a costume, don't worry. Just come as yourself."

Amber slipped into the bathroom. She was texting Lottie that Kelly B. had looked at her like she was a pathetic shelter dog who needed to get adopted when Jessie came in. She pulled out her phone, too, and they traded small smiles. Amber noticed that she'd painted her toenails blue, with little flower decals. Like a secret burst of happiness peeking out from her Birkenstocks.

"Pretty," Amber said, pointing.

"Thanks." Jessie ducked her head, her curtain of hair swinging across her face. But not before Amber saw her smile again.

"Did you do them yourself?" When Jessie nodded, Amber found herself wanting to make her smile some more. "My feet are so ugly! Like horror-movie level. Like, Attack of the Ten Terrifying Toes."

Jessie laughed. She did a little texting, then hoisted her backpack.

"See you, Amber."

"Are you going to the caf?"

"Library." Jessie started for the door. "Mr. Barrow lets me eat there."

Everyone knew that when you needed a place to hide out or decompress, the library—with its plants and pillows and stuffies that, even though this was middle school, you were welcome to hug—was the place.

Still, every day? For a moment, Amber considered going after Jessie and asking her to sit with her. With Lottie absent, how was she ever going to eat all the chocolate pudding Miss Luna supplied? But Jessie would probably just say no, and it would be awkward for both of them, and really, wasn't it better not to ask? Better just to let things be?

• • •

That night when Mariah called, Amber gushed every Lucas detail, including how, when he leaned close, she swore he smelled like apricots. What seventh-grade boy smelled that good?

"When he laughs?" she said. "It's like raindrops on a window. You just want to snuggle into the sound."

"Ode to Lucas!" Mariah cried. "It's about time that boy noticed you. Too bad it took a disaster."

Amber's laugh caught in her throat. Wait. Was that why Lucas was being so nice to her now?

"I predict he'll make a move at the party," Mariah said.

"What's that supposed to mean?"

"Just wait and see. Meanwhile, guess what? My travel team is having a bake sale for you. I'm going to bake cookies and not just any cookies, either. My mom is buying this special dark chocolate from Belgium and we're going to individually wrap each one and tie it with a ribbon."

Amber shut her eyes. She could almost see the cookies, see Mariah tying the pretty ribbons, see her happily collecting the money.

"That sounds like a lot of work, Ri."

"Not if it's for you."

Amber's Second Lie

After she said goodbye to Mariah, Amber went into the kids' bathroom, locked the door, and called Gage. When he didn't answer, she waited and tried again. Still no answer. Gage never let his phone out of his sight, so she knew he was ignoring her. Maybe he was afraid she'd hassle him about the cigarette lighter and his mystery friend. The third time, he finally picked up.

"I can't talk now," he said. "Dad and I are watching a game."

"Just one second, okay? It's the fundraiser. It's happening. I know you told me to stop it and I'm really sorry but by the time I spoke to the committee, people had already started donating." She cleared her throat. Lying to someone you loved—who knew it could be this hard? She steadied herself against the bathroom countertop and rushed on. "And once people donate, it's hard to get their money back. Like, practically impossible."

Amber bit her lip. She had no idea if this was true or not.

"Really?" Gage said.

"So the people who've donated would probably lose all their money."

Gage went quiet.

"I'm sorry." Looking up, she caught her reflection in the mirror and spun away. "I'm really really sorry."

"Okay," he said then. "I get it."

"I'm so stuck. Like, La Brea Tar Pits–level stuck. You're the only one who can convince Dad. If he knows you want this, he might say okay. And I know you don't want it, Gager, but please? Do this for me?" Wait! That sounded so wrong! She tried again. "Not just for me. It would be a huge help for all of us. It would help the whole entire family."

She was out of words. She waited.

"Gotta go," he said then, and hung up.

Less than an hour later, Dad called to say he approved the Price of Kindness.

Approved was too strong a word. More like *allowed*.

After she thanked him two million times at least and they said goodbye, Amber threw herself onto the featherbed futon. She waited to feel happy. And she did. She did!

Except she also felt like she'd swallowed a chunk of sidewalk and it had settled on top of her heart.

She couldn't believe she'd lied to Gage.

She told herself she'd done the wrong thing but for the

right reason. Wrong wasn't always *totally* wrong, was it? If it accomplished good in the end? Maybe truth was beauty, but did that mean less-than-truth was ugly? There were shades of things. Degrees of things! Sometimes you needed to listen to your brain more than your heart.

Right?

Amber turned on the lavender mister and tried to take a calming breath. Truth was turning out to be way more complicated than she'd thought.

Choke

When Amber got to the cafeteria the next day, newspapers were stacked by the entrance, and people were grabbing them as they went in. She took one, then hesitated. Yesterday, with no Lottie, she'd sat at a table of random kids who did homework or puzzles or drew. They'd been glad to share her extra desserts, but still, the thirty-five minutes had dragged on forever.

Where should she sit today? Stalling, she looked at the newspaper. And saw the front-page story.

SEVENTH GRADER'S FAMILY TESTED BY TRAGEDY

An exclusive interview by Melissa Thom

Unlike the adult reporter, Melissa had gotten all the facts right. Not only that. She'd turned Amber's story into a sort of fable, like the ones they were studying in ELA. The fable of the ordinary boy who turned out to be an extraordinary hero. The moral would be: *Do not underestimate the power of love.* Or: *You never know till you do.* Or...

Amber jumped when Kelly B. tapped her shoulder.

"Sit with us?"

"Really? I mean, thanks! I'll just grab some food."

When Amber, her tray piled with extras, approached the table, everyone was reading the newspaper.

"Holy moly," Justina was saying. "Melissa is *such* a good writer. Listen to this: 'Amber Price comes from a close and loving family. Humility runs deep. Describing her courageous brother, Amber calmly but firmly said, "Gage has always been amazing... Everyone is calling him a hero now but guess what? He's always been a hero to us."'" Justina crushed the paper to her chest. "I am reduced to mush!"

"Melissa is so genius," Zara said. "Too bad she wears that lipstick."

"I know!" Kelly W. said. "It's like, did you raid your grandmother's makeup or what?"

"Anyway," Mei said, "I bet she'll have her own news show someday."

Kelly B. scooched over, patting the space beside her. As Amber sat down, all conversation ground to a halt. For a second. Till everyone started talking at once.

"Amber, I can't even imagine."

"I don't even *want* to imagine!"

"Your brother is a demigod."

"My brother would've saved his game controller, forget about me."

"My sister? She wouldn't cross the street to save me!"

Laughing, they began trying to outdo each other with how horrible their siblings were. Justina shook her newspaper.

"This is my favorite part." She read, "'The Confetti Club is sponsoring a fundraiser for the devastated Price family. President Selena Hernandez says, "At Cloverville Middle, when one of us is in trouble, we all are. We hope everyone will do their part. No donation is too small." As for quiet, unassuming Amber, when this reporter asked what it was like to lose all she owned, she replied, 'My family lost everything, but we still have each other.'"

Group sigh. All eyes turned to Amber who, out of nervousness, took a way-too-big bite of her burger, which was dry and crumbly and impossible to swallow. Tears spurted. She felt her face turn scarlet.

"Okay?" Kelly B. patted her back. "Amber, are you okay?"

She nodded, managing to choke down the meat, then waved one hand in front of her face and grabbed her milk carton with the other. She took a gulp and, mortified, attempted a joke.

"My mom, sister, and I are staying with relatives and they're vegetarian. This is my first bite of meat in forever and I got a little overenthusiastic."

Mei and Justina laughed politely, but Kelly W. looked puzzled.

"Your mom and your sister? What about your dad and brother?"

"They—they're staying in an apartment." Amber took another sip of milk. "Just, you know, temporarily."

"Ugh. That has to be rough! Your family sounds so superclose!"

"Meanwhile," Mei said, "it's cool that your relatives are vegetarian. I'm vegan."

"Mei eats so healthy," Zara said. "She makes us feel like prehistoric omnivores."

"I just care about the planet!" Mei said.

"Know what I care about?" Zara said. "Chili dogs! Bubblegum ice cream!"

Mei balled up her napkin and threw it. As a napkin fight broke out, Amber exhaled, relieved not to be the center of attention. Not to mention, not to be asked any more about her family. She folded the wrapper back around her treacherous hamburger. This time, when Kelly B. smiled at her, it seemed almost genuine.

"Amber Price, I decree you're sitting with us from now on."

You Can Be a Hero To!

For the rest of the week, Lottie and Amber texted, their messages issuing from separate galaxies.

Lottie: **poor james has jaundice on top of everything else**

Amber: **lockdown drill, got to be next to lucas who's always buzzing his lips—it's for his ambusher??**

Lottie: **embouchure—for his trumpet! wonder if it affects his kissing abilities**

Amber: **i'll never know**

Lottie: **things so dire here, isla is actually exhibiting human-like behavior toward me**

Amber: **ate lunch at kelly b's table again omg**

Lottie didn't answer that last one.

Mariah, on the other hand, wanted to hear everything about sitting at the premier lunch table. When Amber said she was surprised by how nice everyone was to her, Mariah puffed a breath. Why shouldn't they be? They were the lucky ones to have Amber sit with them. Besides, who said being popular meant you were mean? That was such a cliché.

Mariah said not to worry about a costume for the party. She was taking care of that.

• • •

The school hallways were wall-to-wall with Confetti Club posters.

A red-marker heart with THE PRICE OF KINDNE$$ in the center.

A terrifying drawing of fire destroying a building and the words YOU CAN BE A HERO TO! DONATE TODAY!

Beautiful calligraphy spelling out *Be kind whenever possible. It is always possible.* —*The Dalai Lama*

Amber needed to thank Gage for convincing Dad. Thank him and make sure they were good. She didn't want to do it over the phone. She wanted to see him in person. He'd gone back to school and tomorrow, Friday, he was returning to work at the Convenient Mart. After she took Homer for his nighttime walk, after she cleaned up his poop, which tonight featured a LEGO man, after she listened to Ernie practice her oral presentation on Temple Grandin, a scientist who, among her many amazing accomplishments, invented ways to make slaughterhouses more humane—after all that, Amber went in search of Mom.

The door to her aunt and uncle's room was ajar. When

Amber peeked in, she saw her mother sitting cross-legged in a big, comfy armchair, working on the laptop Aunt Nor had bought her. The sight gave Amber an eerie feeling. Her mother looked different. It was like some younger, brighter Mom hovered in her place.

"I'm hiding out," she whispered. "Come on in."

Amber plucked a pair of socks off the chair's arm and perched beside her mother, who tilted the laptop so she could see.

"I'm trying to learn this graphics program. It's breaking my brain!"

Mom's art had always been about touchable things: ribbons, feathers, fabric, every kind of paper. She loved different textures, smooth or rough, satiny or bumpy. She was a ninja with the X-Acto knife and the hot-glue gun. So it was strange, now, to watch her manipulate colors and images on a flat screen.

"At first I just wanted to get involved because Aunt Nor says the incumbent mayor is a greedy maggot. I said I'd try to help his opponent, Shontel Bibb, with her election materials. But the more I fool around with this..." Her voice drifted off as she shaded a sky-blue background to deep indigo, then violet.

Amber watched, pretending to be interested, till it

seemed possible this other-mother had forgotten she was even there.

"Mom? Could you drive me to see Gage tomorrow after school?"

"Tomorrow?" Younger Mom faded. Familiar, Always A Bit Sad Mom slid back into place. "I promised to go with Aunt Nor to write campaign postcards tomorrow afternoon." She tucked a strand of hair behind Amber's ear. "I'm sorry, sweetie. I know you miss him."

"I can take the bus."

"The bus? I guess that might work." Mom pinched her lower lip. "Uncle Neither is working at home so he can keep an eye on the kids. We could figure out the bus schedule and you could text me when you get there and back home."

"Great! Thanks!"

"You are such a good sister. Gage will be tickled to see you."

Amber hoped both things were true.

Mart

The Convenient Mart was a few blocks from their old house, in a small shopping strip with a Laundromat, an arts supply shop, and a rug store whose sign still said GOING OUT OF BUSINESS though it had been closed forever. When they'd lived in this neighborhood, Amber would sometimes stage a surprise attack on her brother at work. His boss, Mr. Taherian, didn't like "fraternizing on the job," and Gage had outlawed her coming. But if he stepped out on his break to find her sitting on the bench by the door, he'd slip back inside and get another bag of chips, another can of pop. Amber would sip her root beer and snort-laugh as Gage told stories about bizarre customers, like the woman who came in every day for one banana, or the guy who stood by the beer cooler warning people that alcohol was the devil's work.

Now, as she crossed the parking lot, afternoon sun glinting off the cars, she saw a teenage girl sitting on the bench. She wore combat boots and gloves with no fingers. A sketchbook was open on her lap, but instead of drawing, she had her eyes on the mart's door, which kept opening and closing as customers went in and out. A pregnant woman with a box of diapers, two boys tearing open their bags of candy. When a white-haired woman with a walker struggled with the door, the girl jumped up to help. Her sketchbook tumbled to the ground and Amber picked it up.

"Thank you." The girl tugged her knit beanie down. For a moment, she looked as if she'd say more, but instead she positioned herself in the middle of the bench, so there was no way Amber could sit there too.

Clouds were drifting across the sun and Amber pulled Mariah's jean jacket closer. She texted Mom that she'd arrived. She was debating going inside and risking getting Gage in trouble with his boss when the door opened once more and there her brother was, wearing his mart apron over his hoodie. He stopped in his tracks.

"Amber, what the freak are you doing here?"

"So lovely to see you too."

"Did Mom bring you?" His eyes flicked toward the girl on the bench, then across the parking lot. "Is Mom here?"

"I took the bus."

"What? By yourself?"

"Yes by *myself*."

"She's not a baby!" They both turned as the girl on the bench stood up. "I was taking buses by myself when I was six," she said.

Gage tried to swallow his smile, but no use. Huge—huge—goofy grin.

"Excuse me, but I don't believe we asked your opinion," he told the girl. Who ignored him and turned to Amber.

"I'm Ceecee. And you're Amber? You seem perfectly normal, even nice." She had a slow, pretty smile. "Are you sure you're related to this guy?"

"Unfortunately."

When Gage and Ceecee started play-fighting, her sketchbook tumbled to the ground again, and Amber picked it up again. She couldn't believe this. Was Ceecee Gage's girlfriend? Her brother had a secret girlfriend?

Secret Ceecee. Whose hand, Amber saw when she reached for her sketchbook, had homemade tattoos on two fingers. One a crescent moon, one a mini-paintbrush.

"You're an artist?" Amber asked.

"Not really."

"Ceecee's amazing," Gage said. "Come on, show Amber one of your drawings."

Ceecee's nose was already pink with cold, but now her cheeks turned rosy, too. She flipped to a drawing of a plate glass window with a GOING OUT OF BUSINESS sign. The rug shop next door. Shafts of light fell through the glass onto the dusty, once-beautiful-now-faded rugs spread on the floor.

"Oh." Amber caught her breath. "I feel so sorry for the rugs!"

Ceecee shot her a quick, grateful look, then slapped the book shut, as if she'd given away a secret and already regretted it. "I better go."

"Hang on." Gage pulled a pack of cigarettes from his mart apron and slid it into the pocket of Ceecee's jacket. He touched his nose to hers. "Last time," he told her. "You promise, right?"

"I promise!" she said. "I swear."

The mart's door opened again and all three of them jumped as Gage's boss, Mr. Taherian, barreled out. It was illegal for anyone under twenty-one to buy cigarettes, so Gage had to be stealing. Had Mr. T. seen Gage take the cigarettes? Ceecee and her army boots were already trucking across the parking lot.

"Gage, your little sister has come to visit!" A big bear of a man, Mr. Taherian smiled at Amber.

"Yeah. Sorry, Mr. T. She's just about to go."

"It is a blessing to see you again!" Mr. Taherian clapped a hand over his heart. "I told Mrs. Taherian, we had a Dyjhicon in our midst all this time and never knew it. You've heard of a Dyjhicon?" When Amber shook her head, he said, "In the legend, he is a fellow everyone thinks is a timid mouse but in the end proves to be a great hero!" He threw his arms wide. "You are too skinny like him. I will be right back."

As soon as Mr. T. went back inside, Gage whirled on Amber. "You can't tell Mom or Dad about Ceecee."

"Why? Because she smokes and you steal for her?"

"She's quitting." He ran a hand up over the back of his head. Did he know it was the exact same thing Dad did when he was upset? "She's trying. But it's an addiction and it's hard."

"Hmm." Amber tapped her foot. "What else? How do you know her?"

"She goes to the art supply place and sometimes afterwards she comes into the mart. I noticed her, like, months ago, but she never even looked at me. I thought." He squinted at the parking lot like she might magically reappear. "But it turns out she liked me, too, I guess. I mean, yeah. So, the day I came to talk to Mr. T. about starting work again, she stopped into the store. She said, 'Hey, aren't you that guy from the fire?' And I don't know, things just started clicking."

"You've only known each other a little while?" Amber was confused. "You act like you've been together forever."

"I told you, I noticed her a long time ago. And it turns out she was noticing me, too." He looked bewildered and helpless. He looked like somebody in love.

Amber's brain slipped a gear and she was seeing Lucas's dark eyelashes, hearing him buzz his soft lips, breathing in his apricot smell. A shiver that had nothing to do with the chilly afternoon went through her. Not that she was in love with Lucas! But still, she thought she understood. Love could do things to you. It could sweep you up like a warm wind and land you someplace you'd never been.

Aack! Get a grip! she told herself, and frowned sternly at her brother.

"She shouldn't smoke and you shouldn't steal for her. She shouldn't ask you to."

"She doesn't ask me."

"But she takes the cigarettes. That's the same thing."

"Hey, are you Gage Price?" A short, round man roughly Dad's age approached them. "You are, aren't you? I read about what you did. Man, that took guts. Okay if I shake your hand?" Before Gage could answer, he grabbed it. "I thought you were taller. I pictured you a big dude."

"Yeah well, sorry."

"Ha! Score one for the little guys! Seriously, honor to meet you. I plan on donating to your fundraiser." He pumped Gage's hand a few more times before he went into the store, just as Mr. Taherian trundled out with two bags of groceries.

"Thank you so much." Amber took the bags, which weighed approximately a thousand pounds. Mr. Taherian patted her cheek and went back inside.

"Are you sure you're okay taking the bus back?" Gage asked.

"Didn't you hear what your girlfriend said? I'm not a baby."

"Seriously. You know Dad wouldn't like her."

Tattoos, cigarettes—Gage was right.

"Okay. I promise not to say anything to anybody. And Gage?"

He had his hand on the door. "What?"

"Thanks for talking Dad into the fundraiser. It's going to be a really good thing, I promise."

Her brother's eyes clouded over. Something, something like smoke, rose up inside him.

"Be careful on the bus," he said. The door swung shut behind him.

Back to the bus stop, feet trudging but heart skipping. Gage had a girlfriend. A complicated one, but still. Anyone could see how much she liked Gage, which proved her superior judgment. Waiting in the bus shelter, Amber watched a pigeon peck at a candy wrapper on the sidewalk. Ceecee could draw that, she thought. She'd make you see that the pigeon was sort of pitiful but also beautiful, just like those faded, unwanted rugs.

Amber would keep her brother's secret. Of course she would! She'd do whatever he asked, from now on till forever.

Special

She had to wait half a century for a bus, and then it seemed to stop at every corner. By the time she got back, arms limp from lugging all those groceries, Mom and Aunt Nor still weren't home, so Uncle Neither was more than happy to turn the mart food into dinner. Clancy and the little twins took a break from being vegetarians to make lunch meat sandwiches while Amber and the big twins ate the hummus and pita chips. Uncle Neither forced everyone to eat at least one baby carrot before they tore into the boxes of snack cakes.

On Sunday night, Amber marched herself to the guest room, determined to do her math. But when she opened her planner, her heart dropped. She'd forgotten she had a math test tomorrow. She always studied with Lottie, meaning, Lottie always tutored her. A pinch of guilt. She'd let the whole day go by without once checking on her friend.

Amber: **k?**

Lottie: **james home tomorrow, being held hostage 1 more day**

Amber: **lucky u missing math test**

Lottie actually loved math tests, but for Amber's sake, she pretended to hate them.

Lottie: **Yeti sent my work. Sorry can't help u study**

Amber slid her pendant side to side. She still hadn't told Lottie about the Halloween party. Not telling wasn't exactly a lie, but it wasn't exactly the truth either, especially when the person you weren't telling was someone you usually told everything.

Amber typed: **Got to study. Miss u like** She hesitated, then typed: **popcorn misses salt** and turned her phone off before she could see Lottie's response.

Mrs. Oluonye was absent the next day. The sub, a youngish guy in a T-shirt that said *I teach, what's your superpower?*, did not exactly possess good management skills. Maxwell swore on his great-grandmother's grave that Mrs. O. allowed them to play music on their phones during home base. Tyler and his fellow goonies played trash-can basketball. The kids who always got nervous when someone acted out got nervous, and Amber desperately tried to prepare for the math test.

Maxwell was doing what even Amber had to admit was a hilarious imitation of Taylor Swift when the PA crackled and the principal's voice came on. Usually, Mrs. Stefanski left morning announcements to Mr. Monaghan. She only addressed the students for depressing events like lockdown drills or state testing. Everyone quieted down.

"Cloverville Cougars!" Mrs. Stefanski said. "Please give me your full attention. This morning we have an important announcement from Selena Hernandez, president of the Confetti Club. Selena?"

More crackling, then Selena.

"Thank you, Mrs. Stefanski. The Confetti Club has incredible news to share. As of this morning, the Price of Kindness is already closing in on our goal of seven thousand dollars. So far, we have pledges of five thousand seven hundred eighty-two dollars and fifty cents. Can I get a big Cougar roar?"

Everyone roared. The sub flattened himself against the whiteboard like he was caught in a high wind.

"Donations are pouring in from around the community," Selena went on. "Our school project has spread all over town. That is the power of kindness. I have another exciting announcement to make. We are partnering with the high school to do our Price of Kindness presentation at the homecoming game next month. We hope everyone will be there to celebrate when we give the Price family our gift. Meanwhile, keep those donations coming. Spread kindness like confetti!"

Crackle crackle.

"Thank you, Selena," Mrs. Stefanski said. "And thank you, Cougar family, for demonstrating the powerful impact young people can have on our world. I have been proud of this school many times over my career but never more than today. Keep up the amazing work and let's all have a spectacular day!"

When the bell rang, the sub sighed like it was a gift from heaven. Chairs scraped, backpacks zipped, and people spilled into the hallway. Amber had first period in the room, but when she got up to change to her assigned seat, Maxwell loomed in her path. He stuck out his foot.

"Could you please move?" she said.

"Who, me?"

"I don't want to step on your foot, Maxwell."

"I don't want to step on your foot, Maxwell." He pitched his voice high and quivery.

"Max, give it up, man." Lucas suddenly appeared behind Maxwell.

"Like anyone's talking to you, Mucus?" But Maxwell pulled his foot back, then flipped Amber the finger. "Some people think they're special." He pushed past Lucas, bumping his shoulder.

"Don't mind him." Lucas pulled Amber aside and dropped his voice. "He's got his own stuff going on."

She felt shaky but tried not to show it. "What do you mean?"

"He lives on my street. His family...they're kind of messed up. His big brother just got sent to juvie." Lucas made a face. "Ugh. I shouldn't have said that. I'm pretty sure Max doesn't want people knowing."

"I won't tell anyone." Another secret to keep.

"Think about it," Lucas said. "Your brother's a hero and his is locked up. That bites."

"I didn't know."

"It's great about all that money." Lucas smiled. Apricots! She definitely smelled apricots. "That's called amplitude. Or maybe Amber-i-tude."

The bell rang, saving Amber from melting into a puddle on the classroom floor.

The Return of Lottie

The next morning, Lottie was so late getting to their meeting-corner that Amber and Mariah almost gave up on her. When she finally appeared, half running, half staggering, her hair was flat on one side and poofy on the other, and her favorite gray shirt had a large wet stain down the front. Amber took her viola, which Lottie was in serious danger of dropping, as she tried to flap the shirt dry.

"Leon spilled his cereal on me and nothing else was clean. You don't even want to know about the state of my underwear!"

"You are one hundred percent right about that," Mariah said.

"I can't wait to get to school. Give me rules. Give me schedules. Give me an endless sea of boredom!"

The sidewalk was only wide enough for two, and Lottie fell in behind them. The teachers had emailed all her assignments, she said, and she'd done all the work in a matter of hours.

"I calculated that means the entire school week could actually fit into a total of three and a half hours not counting PE, which of course I don't count."

"Not everybody could do the work as easily as you, Ms. IQ." Mariah was walking faster than usual. "Besides, who goes to school just to learn?"

Lottie, still flapping her shirt, had trouble keeping up. When Amber slowed down, Lottie flashed a grateful smile.

"You look so cute," Lottie said. "You look different. Sorry—that came out wrong."

"This is Mariah's jean jacket. And shirt. She's become my personal stylist."

"I thought you didn't like pink. But Mariah knows best." Lottie smiled. Amber drew a breath.

"Something I need to tell you before we get to school. Since you've been gone, I've been eating at Kelly B.'s table."

"You already told me that." Lottie pretended to examine Amber's neck. "Doesn't look like they sucked too much blood."

"That is so judgmental," Mariah called over her shoulder.

"It would be kind of rude if I suddenly stopped sitting with them." Before Lottie could answer, Amber added, "So you have to sit there today, too, okay?"

"They didn't invite me."

"You don't have to be invited! I mean, you sort of do, and I'm inviting you."

"Any time today!" Mariah called back.

"Speaking of inviting." Amber pulled another breath.

She hoped she wouldn't hyperventilate. Why was this so hard? Really, it wasn't as if she'd done anything wrong. "Kelly B. invited me to her Halloween party. It's on actual Halloween."

That glued Lottie's feet to the sidewalk. She glanced at Mariah's retreating back, then gave Amber a *she's-invited-too?* look. Amber nodded.

"Okay." Lottie dug the toe of her sneaker into a crack in the sidewalk. "So. So I guess the three of us aren't going trick-or-treating together this year."

"Lot! We'd already decided we were too old."

"Correction. We *discussed* that. We didn't decide for sure."

The first bell started ringing. Up ahead, Mariah spun around, hands on hips.

"Do you two want us to be late? Did you forget how school works?"

The look on Lottie's face said *maybe*.

Amber had failed the math test. She'd already seen her grade online, but her heart still slid into her shoes when she got her paper back. On top were the dreaded words *See me*.

When the bell rang, she dragged herself to the front of the room. Lottie waited for her by the door. Lucas put his stuff in his backpack in slo-mo. The Yeti got right to the point.

"Ms. Price, your grasp of reflexive and transitive properties is weak. That's making it difficult to move on. I'd like you to start staying after school for extra help."

"I have to get driven to school now and it's hard for my mother to manage." The truth but also a fib. If Mom knew, she'd figure out a way to get Amber to tutoring. But Mom had enough worries already. "And my father..." How could she admit that her parents were separated, that her famously close family had split up and her father lived half an hour away from her? "He works a lot of different shifts."

"Uh—" Lucas said, but before he could go on, Lottie stepped forward.

"I can help Amber. We can work in the library at lunchtime."

"Thank you, Ms. Jackson. You'd be an excellent tutor." Mr. Getty stroked his beard. "What do you say, Ms. Price?"

What *could* she say? She was trapped. Amber had never hated math more than at this moment. Stingy math that only allowed one answer, bully math that never missed a chance to make you feel miserable! She watched Lucas sling his backpack over his shoulder and leave the room. What had he meant to say? Would he have offered to help her, if Lottie hadn't beaten him to it?

"Ms. Price?"

"That would be...great," Amber mumbled.

"Excellent. I'll arrange it with Mr. Barrow. You can start today." The Yeti picked up his pen, sealing Amber's doom.

Traitor

Amber had forgotten her promise to make Clancy a Halloween costume, but her little sister definitely had not. That night at dinner, she announced that she was going to need horns. *Real* horns.

"And hoofs," she said. "Musk oxes have hoofs of steel."

"How about being a black cat?" Amber tried. "Or an evil clown?"

Clancy was outraged. "Those are so genetic!"

"She means generic and she's right," Bert said (by now, Amber could easily tell her and Ernie apart). "Musk ox all the way."

"Are you volunteering to make the costume?" Amber demanded.

"Me?" Bert looked horrified. "I am the only kid in the history of elementary school to fail fourth-grade art!"

But Ernie slipped away from the table and returned solemnly bearing a helmet with—really? Horns!

"From my Viking project," she said.

When Clancy put the helmet on, it slid down over her brow, but she was delighted. "Now I need fur!"

"I know just the thing," Aunt Nor said. "I have an old mohair throw in the attic." She held up a finger. "Proving yet again, never throw anything away."

"I could make hooves," Mom said. "Only for your hands, though. You need to wear regular shoes on Halloween night."

Clancy ran around the table bellowing while the little twins chased her with invisible rifles, Aunt Nor yelled that no weapons were allowed in this house, Homer took the opportunity to steal one of Mom's popovers, and Ernie smiled a rare, radiant (but somehow still solemn) smile. No arguing, no tension, no scolding or I-told-you-so when Bacon tripped and hit his head on the wall. Mom helped him up, kissed his brow, then began unsetting the table. Earrings hopped behind her, weepy-eyed, hoping for leftover veggies.

It's like we live here, Amber thought. Like, we're not just visiting but this is actually our family now. The thought made her jump up from the table. They were getting so comfortable here. Too comfortable. She pulled on the pink denim jacket, got Homer's leash, and took him for a long walk, all the way to the gates of the park. Aunt Nor's neighborhood had fewer streetlights, and there were more stars. That was wrong—the same stars shone down on everyone! But here, they seemed bigger and brighter.

She scooped up Homer's business, which tonight featured a puzzle piece.

Back in the warm kitchen, Mom and Aunt Nor were perched on stools at the island, with laptops and mugs of tea.

"FYI," Aunt Nor said. "You are the child of a genius. And I do not mean your father."

"Noreen!" Mom said.

"Seriously. Besides the graphics for Shontel's campaign, your mom's going to create a logo for the chess club and flyers for the food pantry. Soon she'll have a portfolio and can start making the big bucks."

"My sister has my life figured out."

Homer was slurping water, getting as much on the floor as in his mouth. Amber mopped it up, then made herself tea and sat on a stool, too. She looked at her mother's screen.

"Mom? What about your craft business?"

Her mother moved the cursor a few times before she answered.

"I made so little money. Like Dad has said all along—it was more of a hobby than a business. Now I've lost all my supplies, plus I have to figure out how to pay back my customers for orders I can't deliver." She rested her hands in her lap. "I need to get practical."

"But you love making pretty things!"

"I can still make pretty things." Mom pressed her lips together. "And maybe I can make a living, too."

"Babycakes," Aunt Nor said, "your brilliant mom's taking lemons and making limoncello."

"What even is that?"

"Grown-up lemonade and it's scrumptious."

Mom had finally gotten a new phone and now it began to ring. Nosy Aunt Nor peeked at the screen.

"Gus," she said. "Let it go to voicemail."

Mom rolled her eyes and left the room. Aunt Nor bustled around, making a plate of cookies that she set in front of Amber.

"How are *you* doing?" she asked, and before Amber could answer, she held up a finger. "Don't you dare say fine."

"Some days, everything is awful. Some days, nice things happen."

"And some days it's both. Welcome to life!" Aunt Nor ate a cookie, then fed one to Homer. "What else?"

"No offense, Aunt Nor, because you've been so good to us, I mean beyond good." Amber ran a finger around the rim of her mug. "But..."

"But you wish your parents would get back together and you could get the heck out of here."

Amber nodded. Her aunt gently scratched Homer's head.

"Amber, you and I both know, things weren't perfect before."

Aunt Nor was a sharp pin. Amber was a balloon.

"It's true, they argued." The words whooshed out of Amber. "But they'd always make up."

"Because of your mom. She's good at forgiving." Aunt Nor frowned. "Maybe too good."

Could that be true?

"She just wants us all to be happy," Amber said. *The same thing I want.*

"Well, she deserves to be happy, too."

Amber was a traitor. She'd given her aunt more ammunition against Dad. But she loved her father, who was a wall you could lean against, knowing it would never crumble. Aunt Nor only saw Mom's side of things, and that wasn't the whole truth. Before Amber could think how to say all this, Mom came back looking flustered.

"Nor, any way you could pick up the girls after school tomorrow?"

"Anything is possible." Aunt Nor gave the Vulcan salute, then narrowed her eyes. "What's going on, Meg?"

Mom lifted her mug. "The insurance investigators want to question Gage." She set her mug down. Then lifted it up. Then set it back down again, never taking a sip. "Poor Gage."

"Why pick on him?" Amber said. "He wasn't even home when the fire started."

"They're not picking on him," Aunt Nor said. "It's just a formality. But it's a shame. As if he hasn't been through enough, those man-eating sharks will make him relive it all."

"Gus set up an appointment for after school tomorrow."

"Who's taking him?"

"Gus has to work."

"Why am I not surprised." Aunt Nor huffed a breath.

"He says Gage wants to handle it himself. But I'll go with him."

"Me too," Amber said. When her mother frowned, she rushed on, "I'll tease him and punk him so he won't be nervous."

"I'm not sure that's a good idea."

"It's an excellent idea," Aunt Nor said. "In a storm-tossed sea, Amber is our ship's anchor."

This was the trouble with Aunt Nor. One minute she made you angry and the next she made you love her.

Truth and Beauty, Part 2

When Mom picked Amber up from school the next afternoon, Gage sat in the front seat. He wore a button-down shirt and was that actually a *tie*? This was the work of Dad.

The insurance office was downtown and there was a lot of traffic. As usual, Mom drove at tortoise speed and she began to fret that they'd be late, which somehow made her go even slower, like a self-fulfilling prophecy. The only parking spot they could find was two blocks away. Gage's LeBrons slapped the sidewalk as they hurried toward the office. Amber tried to think of something encouraging to say.

"Aunt Nor says insurance adjusters are weasels and man-eating sharks."

He stared at her. "That really makes me feel better."

The office building was all glass and glinting steel. They got off the elevator on the wrong floor, then had to get back on. Amber could smell her brother's sweat. At last the doors opened onto a bright, carpeted space where a stylish young woman looked up from her desk. When Mom apologized for being late, she gave a bored nod, but when she heard Gage's name, she jumped up.

"Gage Price! It's wonderful to meet you. Thank you for coming." She dimpled. "Please come with me. Mr. Thompkins is expecting you."

As Mom started to follow, Gage turned. "I can do this myself."

"Sweetheart. You *will* do it yourself. I'll just be there in case you need me."

"I'll be fine." He didn't look the least bit fine.

"I just want—"

"Quit babying me! I don't need you. I don't *want* you." Turning on his heel, he followed the receptionist down the hall and through a door that shut behind him.

Mom pressed her palms together, touched her fingertips to her lips. Aunt Nor's words came back to Amber. *Anchor,* she told herself. *Be the anchor in the storm.*

"He's right, Mom. I mean, if he can walk through fire, he can answer a few questions." She steered her mother toward some chairs. "The sooner this gets cleared up the better, right? You know what they say. Beauty is truth, truth beauty—that's all you need to know."

"Is that what they say?" Mom gave a weak smile.

They sank into upholstered chairs and flipped through

magazines, till after several centuries, Gage came back, clutching an unopened water bottle. The receptionist's dazzling smile was totally wasted on him. On the way down in the elevator, he opened the bottle and chugged half of it.

"Aunt Nor was wrong. That guy wasn't a man-eating shark." Another chug. "More like a killer whale."

"What did he ask?"

"Stupid stuff. Like what I saw when I got inside the house. How about flames and smoke?" Another chug. "How about my sister trapped in the attic?"

"Oh sweetie!" Mom tried to hug him and this time, he let her.

"Don't worry, Mom. I settled his kettle."

"I'm sure you did."

Stepping out into the gray autumn afternoon. Gage polished off the water and tossed the bottle into a trash can. Glancing back at the glinting office building, he rolled his shoulders like he was trying to shrug off something heavy.

"Can you drop me at the mart?"

"Really?" Mom was hurt. "I was hoping you'd come to Aunt Nor's with us. I'm going to make spaghetti."

"I'm on the schedule."

"Oh for heaven's sake. You sound just like your father."

"What's wrong with that?" he snapped.

By now it was rush hour, and they inched along. Amber

watched Gage power his window up and down, put in his earbuds and take them back out, pull off his tie, check his phone check his phone check his phone. Instead of relieved, he was more jittery than before. She quietly kicked the back of his seat, trying to make him turn around, but he ignored her.

When they finally got to the mart, Ceecee was waiting on the bench, knit beanie pulled low on her brow. Gage threw Amber a look and zipped a finger across his lips.

I know, she mouthed back.

"Sorry, Mom." He turned to their mother. "I didn't mean to be a jerk before."

"You were upset. And I know it's hard for you to speak up for yourself."

"Yeah."

"Well, it's over." Mom gently wiggled his earlobe. "Promise you won't work too hard, okay? You look pale." As he got out of the car, she said, "I love you, sweetie."

He poked his head back in. "Love you too." He pointed at Amber, then shut the door.

As Mom started to pull out of the parking lot, Amber undid her seat belt and twisted around to look out the back window. Ceecee had stood up from the bench. Even with her cap pulled low, Amber could see the worry printed on her face. That small, watchful face.

When Gage pulled off her cap and kissed her, Amber caught a glint of green in Ceecee's hair.

Wait.

While Gage was still in the hospital. In a visitor's alcove off the hallway, a sketchbook on her lap. A girl with streaked hair and combat boots, a girl Amber thought must hate hospitals as much as she did.

A delivery truck pulled up, blocking her view, and she sank back into her seat. Gage said he and Ceecee hadn't gotten together till after the fire, once he returned to work. She couldn't have come to see him at the hospital.

"I'm glad that's over," Mom said with a sigh. "It really rattled Gage." She caught Amber's eye in the rearview mirror. "Is your seat belt on?"

Amber clicked herself safely into place. Her body, anyway. Her mind was flying far away.

Great White Shark

"Everyone in the high school is speculating on who Gage will take to the homecoming dance. At least according to Isla."

Lottie made googly eyes. They were in the library, eating slices of the cafeteria's so-called pizza while working on math. Lottie set down her pencil to pull off a piece of pepperoni and blot it with a napkin.

"Isla says Gage is oblivious," she went on. "She says his humility is refreshing and adorable. She says the bigger a person's ego, the smaller their brain." She popped the pepperoni in her mouth, chewed and swallowed. "Actually, it might be me who said that last part."

The World Book encyclopedias filled a nearby shelf and Amber couldn't help noticing how their spines formed a picture of a great white shark. The only other kid here now was Jessie Morris, sitting alone at a corner table, bent over a notebook, writing. Lottie, who almost never babbled, babbled on.

"Isla says the halftime show will be spectacular. The marching band is going to spell out BE KIND. She said they've been practicing and it's really tricky, especially the B."

Lottie peeled off another piece of pepperoni and started blotting it, crumpling up oily napkins. Amber felt herself getting more and more irritated. Why did Lottie even eat pepperoni if she had grease phobia? It was Lottie's fault that Amber was sitting here in the first place. Why had she let Lottie bully her into level-one math class? Lottie loved math, not her!

"Since when do you and Isla talk so much?"

"Uh-oh." Lottie blinked at Amber's snappish tone. "Am I being boring?"

Amber grabbed her water bottle and took a swig. At the corner table, Jessie had rested her head on her arms. Her neck looked like the stem of a spindly flower. All of a sudden, Jessie's loner-ness irritated Amber, too. This was mean, not to mention totally illogical. What had Jessie ever done to Amber? She took another gulp of water.

"Amber," Lottie said. "Are you hydrating or ignoring me?"

Amber needed—like the tundra needed trees, only did it?—she needed to tell Lottie how confused she was about Gage and Ceecee. How she was afraid her brother had lied to her. How much that hurt. How it made her wonder if he didn't trust her. How that made her feel like maybe she didn't really know him at all.

She stared at the great white shark. She'd lied to Gage

about the fundraiser. But that was different. That was to help their family!

Maybe she was all wrong. Maybe Gage had a reasonable explanation. If there was anyone who could help her think this through, it was sensible, thoughtful Lottie.

But Amber had sworn not to tell anyone.

Instead, she watched her bestie clean her greasy fingers, pull a piece of colored paper from her binder, and begin to crease and fold, unfold and crease again. Lottie did origami with serene concentration, the same way the twins played chess, and usually Amber loved to watch, but not now. She couldn't tell who she resented more, Gage for making her keep his secret or Lottie for making her sit here, but she decided it was Lottie.

"You know what?" She closed the math book. "My brain needs a rest."

"Okay." Lottie looked up, uncertain. "But we haven't gotten much done."

"Come on." Amber shoved the book into her backpack and stood up. "Let's go to the caf."

"What? And sit with them?" Lottie looked as if Amber had suggested jumping into a snake pit. "All they'll talk about is the party. They'll be at fever pitch."

Lottie was right, of course. Carlotta Jackson was always,

unfailingly, infuriatingly, right. Her clever fingers held up a paper flower. Amber slid back down into her chair.

They slogged through math problems till at last the merciful bell rang. Across the room, Jessie sat up and Amber saw that her cheek was crisscrossed pink, just like Clancy's when she woke from a nap. Jessie stood up slowly, pulling her long cardigan around her like armor. From the doorway, Amber watched her pause by their table and pick up the forgotten origami flower. Amber felt a twinge. More like a stab.

Nobody was making flowers for Jessie, who carefully tucked it into the pocket of her backpack.

Magic Night

Mariah had bought their matching costumes online. That afternoon, before they left school, she waited beside Amber's locker as Lottie shrugged on her jacket, hoisted her backpack, and said bye. The minute Lottie was gone, Mariah handed Amber a bag with her costume inside.

"I can't skip practice this afternoon or Coach will lose it, but we'll still have time to get dressed together." Her Emerald City eyes gleamed. "Oh Amboo! If I was going by myself, I'd be flipping-out nervous, but since we'll be together, in twinner costumes..." She made fists and shook them next to her face. "I got us this amazing makeup. Dead-white skin. Black-rimmed eyes. Wait till you see. The countdown till tonight starts *now*!"

But a few hours later, she sent Amber a text with the puke emoji. Coach, who considered soccer more important than anything, including Halloween, had called an extra scrimmage and her mother had a zillion errands she *had* to do on the way home and OMG, Amber better go ahead and get ready by herself. Mariah would be at the party as soon as she possibly could.

Clancy, wearing her musk ox horns, sat on the futon and watched Amber get dressed. Uncle Neither was going to take her and all the twins out trick-or-treating.

"What are you supposed to be again?" she asked.

"A zombie prom queen."

"That's almost as good as a musk ox."

Amber's dress was pink with bright bloody streaks across the top and skirt. A sash said PROM QUEEN in dripping letters, and there was even a withered wrist corsage. The dress was cut lower than anything she ever wore, and it wasn't as if she had a lot to fill it out, but its silky, floaty skirt felt wonderful against her skin. Without Mariah, she didn't have any special makeup, so she just put on a little mascara and lip gloss.

When she was ready, Mom and Aunt Nor made her pose for photos.

"Drop-dead gorgeous!" Aunt Nor said, straightening Amber's tiara. "Hee-hee, get it? Seriously, babycakes. You look scary beautiful." She wrapped Amber in one of her suffocating hugs.

It was a wet, chilly night, and Mom turned on the car's heater. As they neared Kelly B.'s house, Amber's butterflies swelled to bat-size. The car smelled faintly of old apples and the windows were streaked with rain. Little kids were running along the sidewalks, treat bags bulging, parents following. Just last year, Amber and her friends had been happy, sugar-crazed trick-or-treaters, but now—

"Arrived," announced the GPS. Kelly's big house was lit up like an ocean liner on a sea of lawn.

"Dad's going to pick you up."

"He is? Why?"

"What do you mean why? He's your father."

Amber tugged at her neckline, pretty sure it would raise her father's fuzzy eyebrows.

"He'll be here at ten thirty. On the dot, if I know him." Mom touched Amber's cheek. "You do look lovely, especially for a zombie. Have a good time, okay?"

As if you could promise that! Amber dashed through the rain. She was wearing heels and slipped a little on the slate walkway. Through the glass storm door she could see into a wide entryway decorated with crepe paper and orange lights. Lottie's crush, Tyler, wearing boots and a Harley-Davidson T-shirt, swung the door open.

"Whoa." He looked her up and down. "Is that really you, Amber?"

His hair was gelled up, and he had a fake skull-and-crossbones tattoo on one biceps, and all in all he looked ridiculous but also, undeniably, hot. Lottie would swoon. He showed her where to put her jacket, then led the way into a big room with a high ceiling. Music pulsed. Kids sat on the floor, perched on cushy chairs, sprawled on couches—she counted three couches. One wall was floor-to-ceiling windows, and the darkness outside reflected the twinkling lights and flickering jack-o'-lanterns inside. Kelly B., dressed as a black swan, glided over.

"Amber, that costume is amazing!"

"It was Mariah's idea." Amber looked around nervously. "Is she here yet?"

"I don't think so but anyway." Kelly B. flapped a black wing. "You need to have the best time ever, okay? Just forget your troubles. Just—oh no. What are those goonies doing?" She swanned across the room.

Dr. Who and a giant penguin were wrestling over a lighted jack-o'-lantern. Kelly B. tried to take it from them, but it was a big pumpkin and it slipped, hitting the tile floor. *Thunk!* It cracked in two. Somehow the candle inside landed upright, its flame shrinking then shooting up, wafting this way and that in the commotion. Amber took a step backward, bumping into a mad scientist.

"Hey," said the voice of Lucas, and then, "Are you okay?"

It's just a candle, she told herself. *Calm down*, she ordered her skittering heart. Dr. Who was pinching the flame with two fingers, and Kelly B. was fetching a dustpan, and it was all over that quickly, but still. When she answered Lucas, her voice sounded very small.

"It's okay. I'm fine. Hi."

"FYI," he said. "When you're at a party, frowning is against the rules."

"Parties have rules?"

"Oh yeah. Rule number one—drink pop." He led her to a cooler, pulled out a can, popped the tab, and held it out like a waiter in a fine restaurant. "Great vintage. Excellent choice."

"Very funny." She took a sip, but it went down the wrong pipe and she began to sputter. Lucas thumped her back.

"Rule number two, don't choke."

Tugging at her embarrassing neckline, she wished Mariah was here. All the kids were in groups and the music was so loud. Lucas was saying something she couldn't hear. What would she do if he walked away? What would she do if he asked her to dance? How was she ever going to make it to ten thirty?

"Here I am!" Mariah flew across the room. "I'm sorry I'm so late! When I finally got home I was like a swamp rat and I needed an epic shower and then my mother forced me to eat before I came and oh oh oh, look at you, Amboo!"

Mariah's dress was black, the bloody streaks scarlet. Her auburn hair hung loose down her back and the white pancake makeup made her eyes even greener, which should have been impossible. In short, she looked spectacular. She made Amber twirl, the silky skirt floating around her legs.

"My beautiful undead sister!" she cried.

"I'm teaching Amber about parties," Lucas said.

"Well, you're a terrible teacher." She tugged a lock on his fright wig. "Why are you just standing here? You're supposed to dance!"

"That is not in my curriculum," Lucas said.

"What did I tell you? A terrible teacher." Mariah pulled Amber away, then whispered in her ear. "He likes you, Amber Price. Let there be no doubt."

"We were talking, that's all!"

"Would you stop? Tonight is the night, zombie girl! You are reinvented. To celebrate, you are going to do something extremely extreme."

"I do not like the sound of this."

"Get ready to dance with me."

"No! I can't! You know I look like a flamingo on steroids. Plus—in heels? I'll kill myself."

But Mariah was already dragging her into the middle of the room where the furniture had been cleared away, and Amber had no choice. It didn't matter, though, because it turned out nobody cared how you danced. People jumped and spun and wiggled around, throwing down their own moves. Tyler did something he called the Worm, while Zara and Mei did what looked like a very bad audition for *Dancing with the Stars*. Kelly B. went from ballet to hip-hop to robot without missing a beat. Mariah and Amber mirrored each other, stretching high and corkscrewing low, till somebody yelled, "Ride my train!" and they were all linking together, hands on waists, chugging around the room faster and faster, till the beat switched to a slow dance and everyone except official couples collapsed onto the couches and chairs.

Whew.

Mariah got in line for the downstairs bathroom and Amber pulled out her phone. Everyone was taking photos—maybe she would, too. But now she saw she'd missed two calls from Gage. She stepped through French doors onto a wide patio. The rain had stopped and a boy and girl were very busy kissing. Amber headed the other way, out onto the wet grass.

He answered right away.

"Gage, I'm at a party."

"Oh right—I forgot. Dad said he's picking you up. Are you having a good time?"

"As a matter of fact, yes."

"It can't be that good if you're talking to me." A fake laugh.

She pulled off the tiara, which was pinching her temples. "If I call you when I get home, will you promise to answer?"

"I was going to see if you wanted to meet up tomorrow after my shift at the mart. What's that place you like?"

"Koko's!"

"But if your social calendar's too full—"

"I'll be there!"

"Three o'clock." And he was gone.

"Amber?" Mariah leaned out the French doors. "What are you doing? Pizza's here!"

Amber set the tiara back on and hurried inside to the warmth and light. Gage wanted to meet up! He'd even picked Koko's, her favorite. This was not the behavior of a brother who was lying to you, was it? A song she loved was playing and she did a small, personal dance of happiness, then plopped two slices of pizza on her plate.

"Hey," Tyler said. "I thought zombies only ate brains."

"Meaning you're safe, considering you're brainless."

When he laughed, she had to admit, he was very agreeable-looking. Too bad he knew it.

"I babysat my little cousins for you," he said. "They're actual, real-life brain-eaters, but I needed to earn bucks for your fundraiser."

"Really?" She was touched, also embarrassed. "I mean, thank you." Todd's eyes slid down her front and she tugged at her neckline. "By the way," she said, "if you want any babysitting tips you should talk to Lottie."

"Lottie?" He rubbed his cheek. "Lottie Jackson?"

"Uh-huh. You really should talk to her anyway. Not just about babysitting."

"If you say so." He tore into his pizza.

We talked about you, she could tell Lottie when she described the party.

She was sitting on the floor with Mariah when Lucas sat down on her other side. By now Amber had given up on the tiara, Mariah had kicked off her high heels, and Lucas had ditched the mad-scientist wig. They almost looked like their real selves.

"I didn't tell you party rule number seven hundred sixty-two," Lucas said.

"I'm ready."

"Rule number seven hundred sixty-two, share your pizza."

As he stole a slice off her plate, Mariah dug a very sharp elbow into Amber's side.

Kelly B.'s mother tried to organize games, but the only one that caught on was pumpkin piñata. By the time the candy rained down, the party was almost over. Kelly B. handed out glow sticks and everyone ran outside, laughing and shrieking, trailing streams of light through the chilly darkness. When she saw Dad's car drive up—the first parent to arrive, of course—Amber told Kelly B. thank you, then gave Mariah a goodbye hug. As she crossed the front lawn, Lucas caught up to her. He was out of breath and, suddenly, so was she.

"See you, Amber-i-tude!"

"Back at you, Lucas-i-tude!"

She buttoned the pink denim jacket over her dress before she got into the front seat.

"Fancy house," Dad said. "Are these new friends?"

"Uh-huh." Inside the dark car, her glow stick gave off a mystical purple light.

"You're a princess?"

"A zombie."

"For the love of Mike! Should I be scared?"

"Very."

"Thanks for the warning, Lamb."

Now she was glad that Dad had picked her up. He wouldn't ask a lot of invasive questions, the way Mom would have. As they rode along, the heater purring, the glow stick glowing, the air smelling of pine, she felt safe in that way she only did with Dad. She let her eyes drift closed. The car was a cocoon, it was a nest, it was a fortress no enemy could invade.

"I talked to Clancy tonight," Dad said. "She was over the moon about her costume. She said you made it?"

"Everybody helped. Mom, Aunt Nor, even Ernie."

"That's nice. That's good." Something in his voice made her open her eyes. "Remember that year you insisted on being an ostrich? Still can't believe your mother made you that costume."

"What I remember is how you always stole my licorice."

"You didn't want it! You said licorice was the armpit of candy."

"It's true."

At Aunt Nor's the porch light was on and the bedsheet ghosts, wet with rain, drooped from the tree branches. Amber hated to say goodbye. *Come in*, she longed to tell her father, but she knew he'd say it was too late, and she couldn't stand to hear him say that.

"By the way." He gave the air freshener a spin. "How's that fundraiser going?"

"It's so good, Dad. Everyone is super into it." She could tell he still didn't approve, and that made her all the more grateful to him. "Thanks again for saying yes."

"I told your brother I want him to accept the check at the homecoming game. He wants me to do it but come on! He's the hero of this story."

"That'll be hard for him, Dad. Gage is so shy."

"It's time he got over that. Past time. He needs to make a speech saying thank you." Dad smiled at her. "Maybe you can help him write it. Or at least encourage him."

"I can try."

To her surprise, when she got out of the car, so did Dad. Mom must have been watching for her, because she opened the front door as they came up the walk.

"Here's our princess, safe and sound," Dad said.

"I'm a zombie, Dad."

"Nah. You're a princess."

Mom had brushed her hair and put on Amber's favorite earrings, the silver hoops with little stones. A long-ago gift from Dad. Amber hadn't seen her wear them since the night of the fire.

"Thanks for fetching her," Mom said.

"The pleasure is all mine," Dad said.

Could they possibly act any stiffer? Yet something in the way they looked at each other made Amber wonder if this was how it was when they first fell in love. When Dad came to pick Mom up for a date, did he act this proper and shy? Did she gaze at him like *Who is this sweet old-fashioned fellow?*

Could love like that disappear? Or did it get preserved somewhere, like a tiny bug in amber?

She thanked Dad, promised Mom she'd tell her everything in the morning, and ran upstairs. Leaning over the banister, she heard her parents' voices. Dad was still here.

Maybe? Possibly? A fizz of hope. It seemed like a night when magic could happen.

She changed into PJs and curled up on the futon. Opening her phone, she saw dozens of photos from the party, and more were pouring in.

A Change in the Weather

On Saturday, the grass was frosty white and flurries were in the forecast. It was a day for boots, boots Amber didn't have.

But as she got ready to meet Gage, she remembered the donation box shoved into the back of the hall closet. There the boots were, still on top. The gently worn leather was soft and her feet slipped right in. Cinderella, she thought, wiggling her toes. Why had she rejected the boots before? She couldn't remember.

Mom actually drove the speed limit, and they got to the mart just as Gage came out. Mom told them she'd be at the library.

"Meet me there in about an hour, okay?"

Koko's was a little bakery with round tables, pastel-colored posters, and a paw-waving kitty on the counter. Amber, Lottie, and Mariah had met up here approximately a zillion times. Mrs. Cheu, whose hair reminded Amber of a wooly white cap, greeted them with a bow.

"It is so good to see you, Amber Price! I'm so happy you are safe and well. What can I get you?"

Amber asked for her usual mango bubble tea. Gage said he didn't want anything and pulled out his wallet. Mrs. Cheu held up a hand.

"On the house and on the double," she said.

They took a table by the front window. Outside, somebody had hung a pirate's eye patch from the branch of a sidewalk tree. The wind blew empty candy wrappers around.

"Want to see pictures from the party?" she asked. "Some are pretty funny."

The truth was, she'd barely stopped looking at her phone since last night. Though in the end she'd never taken any photos herself, she was amazed by how many she appeared in: dancing, swinging at the jack-o'-lantern piñata, holding up a giant slice of pizza like a fish she'd caught. The one of Kelly B. giving her bunny ears had the most likes. *Amber embraces her happy!* the caption said. Her brother took her phone and scrolled.

"Somebody had a good time." He paused at a photo of Lucas wearing her tiara. "Who's this guy?"

"Nobody," she said, cheeks warming. Gage handed back the phone.

"World's most pathetic liar," he said.

Mrs. Cheu brought Amber's drink and set a dish in front of Gage.

"For you, Mr. Hero," she said.

They both thanked her, but as she walked away, Gage scowled at the plate.

"What the freak is this?"

"A curry puff, I think."

He started pulling the flaky little pillow apart.

"You know what's strange?" she said. "The party was last night but it's already kind of a blur. The photos—it's like they're *becoming* the party. You know what I mean? Like, it's all turning into a story people are telling." She sipped the delicious tea. "It's nice but also kind of unreal."

Gage quit decimating his curry puff and rested his arms on the table. It was like he was wearing his own Halloween mask, the mask of gloom. Amber was sure he'd say he had no idea what she was talking about, or possibly not even answer at all, but instead he nodded.

"Dad said this thing to me once. I'd screwed up again, I don't even remember how, but he was P.O.'d. I mean, deeply, deeply P.O.'d. He told me that I was a loser."

"No he didn't!"

"Actually, he said *big* loser." Gage looked out the window, where fluffy snowflakes were starting to blow around. "Right away, he felt bad. You know how he does that? Says what he thinks, then feels bad and tries to take it back?"

"I thought I was the only one who ever noticed that. He does it to Mom all the time."

"So he tried to take it back, but I couldn't even listen to him. Finally he made me sit down. And I still remember what he said." Gage turned to look at her. "He said, the biggest mistake you can make is letting other people tell you who you are. You're the only one who can decide that."

Amber's phone, lying on the table, kept lighting up with more texts. She slid it into the pocket of Mariah's jacket.

"Aunt Nor said something like that to me." She spooned up boba. "Those two would be shocked to know they agree on something."

"Ceecee left town."

"She did?" Amber choked down boba. "Why?"

"She went to live with her aunt."

"Where?"

"Some other state. Pennsylvania or New York."

"You don't know which one?"

"Her aunt's rich." He hitched a shoulder. "She doesn't have any kids and she's always loved Ceecee. She says Ceecee's so talented, she should go to a private school with a good art department, so she can get into a prestige art college. Her parents hated for her to leave, but they finally gave in. It's...you know." His shoulder fell. "You know. A dream come true for Ceecee."

Amber sat back in her chair. A dream come true for Ceecee, but what about Gage?

"Are you still together?" she asked.

"Nah." He flicked a finger at the shredded curry puff. "Long distance would never work. We decided a clean break is the way to go."

Poor Gage! This was the kind of thing that was always happening to him. He gave his heart to something—making the team, being a boyfriend—but somehow it never worked out.

Breaking up was Ceecee's idea, Amber was sure. Gage was in love. He'd have tried his hardest to make it work.

Still.

"Maybe it's for the best?" She stabbed her tea with her straw. "I mean..."

"What?" He went stiff and alert. "You mean what?"

"Gage, you didn't know her before, did you? Before the fire?"

His face was a screen flashing surprise, then anger. "Where'd you get that idea?"

Mrs. Cheu was back, this time with two cream buns. Gage, who was shy but never rude, ignored her. Amber said thank you three times. When Mrs. Cheu was safely back behind the counter, she leaned toward her brother and lowered her voice.

"I thought I saw somebody who looked like her at the hospital."

His face went dark.

"It was her, wasn't it?" When he nodded, the barest of bare nods, she sat back. "So you two started dating before the fire? Ceecee's why you kept making excuses to go out at night? Okay, all right, I get it. You had to keep her a secret. You were grounded and besides, you didn't need Dad criticizing your girlfriend. You could've told me, Gager." She swallowed. "But anyway. This will sound harsh, but maybe it's okay she's gone. Ceecee's so complicated. I hope you know that every girl in school is dying to go to homecoming with you. Including Isla Jackson."

"Isla." He made a face. "She already asked me."

"She did? I hope you told her yes."

"Why would I do that?"

"You're right." Amber laughed. "Why would you? She's a certified pain in the butt."

The phone in her pocket vibrated again. The story of Kelly B.'s party just kept growing. But Gage was pushing his dish away and standing up.

"We should get going."

Amber wrapped her cream bun in some napkins and stuck it in her other pocket. Outside the snow flew around like it was confused about what it was supposed to do. As they walked toward the library, Amber knew every shop they passed. Revolve Thrift with its window display of secondhand costumes, Sam's Smoke Shop, Arabica Café with its chalkboard advertising pumpkin lattes. They passed the community bulletin board with its flyers for concerts and garage sales and look—a Shontel Bibb poster that Mom had designed! Walking beside her brother, it almost felt like they still lived here. Like, if they went up the hill, past the school and the library, down the street with the big yellow house on the corner, their own house would still be there, Mom's wreath on the front door, their cars in the driveway.

But when Amber caught their reflections in the Laundromat window, she was wearing a stranger's boots, and her brother was ten paces ahead, as if trying to outrun her. Out of nowhere, the boots began to pinch.

"Hey." She caught up and carefully hooked her arm through his injured one. "I'm really sorry about Ceecee. Thanks for telling me. And just so you know—I never breathed a word to Mom or Dad or anybody."

The street sloped upward toward the library, and Gage slowed down. Their breath made little clouds in the cold air.

"There's something else," he said. "Dad says the insurance company is keeping the investigation open."

"The weasels! The great white sharks!" When that didn't make him smile, she tried again. "So what? You already talked to them. You settled their kettle."

At the corner they waited for the light. Snowflakes

drifted like bits of torn paper. When the light changed, she and Gage crossed the street, but at the foot of the library steps, he stopped and pulled his arm free from hers.

"The guy at the insurance company," he said. "Mr. Thompkins. He seemed nice at first. Like he was on my side, like he didn't want to grill me but it was his job and he couldn't help it."

A woman with her arms full of books smiled at them as she hurried past. Gage yanked his hood up over his head.

"Just when I start feeling relaxed, he pulls up this report on his computer. He says that, according to Mom, I was at the library that night. And I say, 'Yeah,' and he says, 'Well, Gage, the library closes at nine. And you got home after ten.' Then he pushes his designer glasses up his nose and looks at me like he freaking feels sorry for me. He says, 'Where were you during that interval?'"

The boots pinched. The air had grown tiny icy teeth.

"I never went to the library. I met up with Ceecee." The words tumbled out of him. "We just walked around. It was a nice night, remember? We hung out. And then I walked her to the bus stop and waited with her. It took forever for the bus to show up, and then I came home."

Amber must have been holding her breath, because now it burst out like the world's most powerful cleansing exhale.

"Did you tell Mr. Thompkins?"

"No way I'm dragging Ceecee into this mess. I told him that after we left the library, my friends and I rode around for a while. Like an idiot I thought he'd let it go. But it turns out he was just playing good cop. He wanted to know the other guys' names." Gage stared over Amber's head. "I said they didn't do anything, I didn't want to get them in trouble. He asked me again and I said it again, and then he gave me this look. He said he hoped I'd think about it some more."

Amber shoved her cold hands into her pockets, accidentally squishing the cream bun. Gage had lied to an investigator. That was a serious lie.

For some reason, Maxwell's sneering face rose in her mind. *You think you're so special?*

"Gage, I get that you want to protect Ceecee, but maybe you're being too..." What was that word? "Too gallant." Was he even listening to her? She couldn't tell. "Maybe you should—"

"I kept thinking Dad would get on me about where I was that night, but he never did, I don't know why." Gage's eyes were tearing up, maybe from the cold but maybe not. "Mr. Thompkins said our conversation was confidential but no way do I trust the guy. What's to stop him from calling Dad and saying, 'FYI, Mr. Price. Your son's been lying his butt off.'"

"It's not fair! Why does anyone care where you were *before* the fire? What does that matter, compared to what you did?" Her own eyes grew hot with tears. "I'm sorry, Gage. I should've put the smoke detector battery back! Only, I was so mad at you for shutting me out. I wish I never went up to your room! It's just, I missed you and I wanted to be near you and—"

"Quit it." He put his arm around her. "Mute it."

"It's all my fault you got hurt. Nobody ever says it out loud, but it's true."

The worst, ugliest kind of crying was when you didn't expect it, when the sorrow inside suddenly grew and swelled till it couldn't be contained and it painfully, messily burst. She leaned against her big brother, burying her face in his hoodie. Gage let her cry, maybe because he could tell she needed to, or maybe because he didn't know what else to do.

"You got it all wrong." How could his voice be this rough and tender at the same time? "Never say any of that again. Promise me, Amberghini."

She reached into her pocket, found the napkin sticky with bun crumbs, and blew her nose. Even if she never said it again, she knew she'd never stop thinking it.

Not You

On Monday morning, Selena caught up with Amber. She was wearing a T-shirt that said *When the power of love overcomes the love of power, the world will know peace.*

"Amber! We made our goal!" A quick, giddy hug. "Actually, we're over it by almost five hundred dollars, with more than a week to go. I wanted to tell you first, before we announce it this afternoon."

It took a moment for the words to sink in.

"I can't even—I mean, thank you," Amber said. "Up to the moon and down to the bottom of the sea."

"I'm blissing out!" Selena said. "No, that came out wrong. I'm sorry for what happened, Amber, but I'm happy for what it proves. Who says we can't make kindness the norm?"

At lunchtime Amber and Lottie sat in the library eating candy they'd stolen from their younger siblings' trick-or-treat bags. When Lottie asked about the party, Amber said it was okay.

"You had a brilliant time," Lottie said.

"I did?"

"Would you please quit dissembling?"

"Okay. It was awkward at first but then it was fun."

"I'll accept that answer." Lottie knocked off a couple of equations. "Anyway, you look amazing in the party photos."

"The dress was so low-cut, and it's not like I have anything to fill it out." Amber began to feel queasy, and not just from all the candy. The party—it had been possibly the best night of her middle school life, but she couldn't really, truly share it with Lottie. Then she remembered. "Tyler asked about you."

"He did not."

"Did."

"You're not just trying to make me feel better?"

"We had a whole conversation about you." She remembered Tyler staring at her neckline. "But really, Lottie. *Tyler?* You are so far above him."

"Do not diss my foolish heart."

Across the room, Jessie sat scribbling in her notebook. Maybe that notebook and whatever she wrote in it kept her company. Somehow this made Amber think of Ceecee and her drawing, and from there it was a quick jump to Gage and where he'd been the night of the fire, and now she realized Lottie had set down her pencil and was peering at her.

Peering like the table between them had grown so wide it was hard to see across.

"What?" Amber said.

"I have bad news. But then again, maybe you'll consider it good news."

"Lot, what are you even talking about?"

"I have to start going to the orchestra room during lunch. It's impossible to practice at home. James has colic, so either he's screaming so loud you can't hear anything else, or he's asleep so we can't make a sound. My solo is a disaster and the winter concert is just around the corner."

Lottie was first viola in the orchestra. Amber could never tell if Lottie liked the viola or was just good at it.

"Plus." Lottie started folding a peanut butter cup wrapper. "Mr. Getty worked his evil icy wiles on me and convinced me to join Mathletes. We're meeting today after school." She pulled a disgusted face, but Amber knew nobody could convince Lottie to do anything. She made all her own decisions.

"The other Mathlete teams will pee their pants in terror," Amber said. "You will crush them."

"I plan on it." Lottie was making the world's tiniest origami dove. "But what this all means is, I've got zero time for socializing. And I can't tutor you at lunch." She grimaced. "The Yeti will no doubt have another suggestion."

"I should just give up and go into regular math."

"No! Why? You can do level one."

"*You* can. I'm not you."

The words hung in the air. Lottie set down her minuscule dove. Amber looked at the World Books, where the great white shark bared its double row of teeth.

"Well, I guess you need to do what you need to do." Lottie slid the math book into her backpack and stood up. Amber could tell Lottie was waiting for her to say something, but no words came. Lottie swung her backpack over her shoulder. "Maybe that's how it is for both of us."

The bell rang. At the door, Amber looked back and saw Jessie once again pause by their table. She picked up the candy-wrapper dove and cradled it in her palm. Something in the way she stood there, shoulders sloping, head bent, was like a warning. Like, this is how awful it is to be alone. This is how terrible it is to be friendless.

Another sickish wave broke over Amber. She spun away, afraid to look at Jessie any longer. Out in the hallway, Kelly B. called to her.

"You missed lunch again!"

"I'll be there tomorrow," Amber promised.

Out of Bad

That afternoon, she walked home with Mariah, who by some miracle didn't have soccer. They grabbed chips, apples, and drinks and went to her room. Mariah pulled up a how-to video for making double-Dutch braids. She ran a comb through Amber's hair.

"This is a trial run. If it works, I'll do it for you for the homecoming game." She tugged on Amber's scalp. "Did I tell you my travel team is coming? We're supposed to have a game that night, but no one plans to miss the Price of Kindness." More tugging. Mariah was ruthless with a comb. "Coach was definitely not happy, but when we explained, he actually got the game postponed. He said life is all about teamwork." Mariah laughed. "Omigod, I need at least four extra hands to do this!" When Amber tried to turn her head to see herself in the mirror, Mariah cried. "Don't move! I'll mess up."

"Mess up! Mess up!" Savannah hopped off her perch and dipped her beak into Amber's glass of guava nectar.

"Speaking of messing up," Amber said. "Lottie and I—we didn't actually have a fight, but I think she's..."

"Pulling away?" Mariah filled in her blank.

"I wasn't going to say that, but—"

"It's not your fault if you're changing."

But Lottie was changing too. Or was she just becoming more who she always was? The truer Lottie? Amber winced as Mariah's comb dug in.

"The fire was a terrible thing," Mariah went on, "but look what's happened as a result. If it wasn't for that night, Gage might've stayed a slacker the rest of his life. Instead he's discovered the hero he was meant to be. And you? You're making all kinds of new friends. You're even getting a new hairstyle!" Mariah laughed. "For real, though. I'm serious. You didn't do anything wrong. The opposite."

Amber's hair was too fine or Mariah was never meant to be a hairdresser, and despite all her pulling and tugging, the braids were a disaster. They switched out the hair video for their favorite yoga teacher and were lying in corpse pose when Mom texted from the driveway. Time to go. Mariah opened her closet and pulled out a shimmery-gold puffer.

"It's too cold for that denim jacket. My nana sent me this, and I already have two others."

"You need to stop giving me stuff, Ri."

"I will once you get all that Price of Kindness money. Oodles of money!"

"Oodles!" crowed Savannah. "Oodles!"

Mariah walked Amber out onto the front porch. Mom, sitting in her car, waved a hurry-up hand.

"Your mom looks like she's doing better," Mariah said.

"She's gotten heavy into working on Shontel Bibb's campaign with my aunt."

"That's so cool. My mom hates the mayor we have now."

"It's a close race, like down to the wire. The vote's tomorrow." Her mother was furiously typing on her phone. "Plus, she's planning to take courses in graphic design at the community college."

"Also very cool."

"It would be a big thing. She never went to college."

"My nana has this saying. 'Out of bad comes good.' Sometimes it makes me want to gag because, come on! Bad can be just plain bad. But." Mariah, the beautiful, strong, self-confident Mariah, suddenly turned shy. "Not to go all mushy and misty, but nothing tragic has ever happened to me or my family. Sometimes I feel like my life is too easy, you know? Kind of...flimsy."

"Easy and flimsy are good, trust me."

"You know way better than me. But I just want to say, this whole thing has taught me so much. Watching how everyone at school has come together, I've been thinking Nana is right. Good does come out of bad. And going through this with you, I feel like our friendship has gotten even closer and more meaningful." She draped the shiny jacket over Amber's shoulders. "Anyway. I'm so glad I can be here for you."

"Me too."

"Wear that jacket tomorrow!"

Nail Biter

Election day dawned bright and cold, making Amber extra grateful for her new golden puffer. Before home base, as they stood at their lockers, Lottie gave Amber the side-eye.

"Cute jacket," she said.

"It's so...gleamy. Also too big."

"It still looks nice."

"Thank you."

Ugh! They sounded like polite strangers.

After school, she and her mother tidied the house, which in the past week had gone from messy to catastrophic. Aunt Nor was hosting a watch party for all the volunteers tonight. She had left before breakfast to distribute literature outside the polling stations. By the time she got home, her cheeks were chapped and her voice was hoarse. The polls closed at seven thirty and the house began to fill with people. In every room, tablets and laptops were tuned to cable news.

"We're going to win this," Aunt Nor croaked as she moved from room to room, patting people's shoulders. "Tonight our work pays off."

Not everyone was so sure, Amber could tell. The returns were too close to call. Someone had put two bottles on the living room mantel. The champagne was for if they won, and the Scotch for if they lost. In the kitchen, Uncle Neither unwrapped trays of food.

"What if we lose?" Amber asked him. "Aunt Nor will be so sad."

"Ballistic is more like it. She doesn't do sad." He handed her a tray of mini-sandwiches stuck with frilly toothpicks. "Thanks for helping out. Where are your sister and no-good cousins?"

"Bert's running data to predict the results. Ernie was freaking a little, so I made her a futon pillow fort. The little demons are down in the basement. I told them they could make one more stealth run for cookies and then they need to get ready for bed."

Her uncle gave her an appreciative look. "How do you do that?"

"Do what?"

"Keep track of us all! You always know who needs what when and how."

"I don't even think about it." Amber shrugged. "I just do it."

"Funny." Uncle Neither's smile was gentle. "Your brother said the same thing about running into a burning building."

As Amber went around offering sandwiches, everyone

seemed to know who she was. If they weren't saying how nice it was to meet her, they were saying they looked forward to homecoming. Heading back to the kitchen with an empty tray, she passed Mom, who was talking to a distinguished-looking man in a suit and tie.

"Terrific," Amber heard him say. "Do you have business cards?"

"Not at the moment." Mom wore the twinkly silver earrings, and tonight she even had lipstick on. "But let me give you my email."

"Will you look at her." Aunt Nor took the empty tray from Amber. "Working the room!"

"I think she's just talking to people."

"Don't underestimate your mother." Her aunt wagged a finger. "She does enough of that herself. Or she *did*."

Looking again, Amber saw that her aunt was right. Mom was shining. The bit of sadness that usually trailed her was gone. Amber had thought she was the only one who'd ever noticed that sadness, but Aunt Nor had, too.

Out of bad comes good. Maybe Mariah's nana was right.

The returns were excruciating. Every time Shontel Bibb pulled ahead, her opponent (aka the maggot incumbent) caught up and retook the lead. One polling place had a glitch with its machines and couldn't report for a while. Homer, banished to the basement for eating off people's plates, set up a mournful howl. Around ten o'clock, Aunt Nor sank into a crumpled heap on the sofa. Her head fell back and she stared at the ceiling, finally giving way to exhaustion. Mom put half a sandwich in her hand.

"Eat," Mom said.

"I can't," Aunt Nor croaked.

Mom tore off a piece and put it in her sister's mouth. Aunt Nor chewed obediently.

"I'm worried, Meg."

Like she'd heard her cue, Bert charged into the room, fist raised in triumph. "I call it!" she cried. "Victory is ours."

"Brittany, my darling." Aunt Nor shook her head. "Thanks for your encouragement. But it's still up in the air."

"Believe, Mom. The force is with us."

Twenty minutes later, the returns took a swerve. Twenty minutes after that, Shontel Bibb was declared the new mayor.

"Celebration" started playing on someone's phone. The champagne cork flew and the glasses filled. (It turned out there were more bottles in the fridge.) Uncle Neither poured Amber a few drops, and everyone toasted: to the new mayor, to the volunteers, to Aunt Nor. Amber sipped, then handed her glass to Bert, who drained it and smacked her lips.

"When I grow up, I'm going to drink lots of champagne." She handed back the empty glass. "Aren't our moms bizarre?"

"For sure. But good-bizarre."

"I better get upstairs. Ernie can't sleep unless I'm there."

"Bert, thanks for being so nice to my family."

"It's easy." Bert laughed and ran up the stairs.

Could two sips of champagne make you tipsy? Or did she feel this way because it was almost midnight, or because the house, full of buzzing bodies, had gotten too warm? Maybe it was watching her mother toss her head and laugh as Aunt Nor did an embarrassing victory dance. When her aunt grabbed Mom's hand, Mom grabbed Amber's, and the three of them spun in a circle.

"So, this is what goes on here." Dad had let himself in without them noticing. He wore his scrubs and a quizzical smile.

"Gus!" Mom pressed a hand to her flushed cheek. "What are you doing here?"

"I saw the news as I was ending my shift." He ran his hand up over the back of his head. He still hadn't gotten a haircut. "I figured I'd say congratulations."

"That's so nice." Mom fanned her face. "Thanks."

"Job well done." Dad actually shook Aunt Nor's hand.

"Good timing," she said. "You can help clean up."

After Dad gave Amber a hug and told her she really needed to get the heck up to bed, after Homer offered him a slimy tennis ball, after Aunt Nor handed him a trash bag which he filled—after all that, Mom took his arm and steered him into the kitchen.

Amber went to the stairs but paused on the bottom step. The air felt charged, like electric particles were flying all around. Like the air was flammable but good-flammable, if there was such a thing. Earrings, who'd been hiding out all night, hopped by and Amber scooped him up.

The fire wasn't fair. Gage getting grilled by the insurance company wasn't fair. The secrets she had to keep from her parents and friends were definitely not fair.

"But it's going to be okay," she whispered to the bunny. It was three days till the Price of Kindness ceremony. Gage would make the speech Dad wanted him to, and everyone would cheer. In the kitchen, Mom laughed. Mom, who'd shone like a star tonight. Mom, who was so good at forgiving. Amber hugged Earrings, who twitched his pink nose.

"It will be okay," Amber whispered. "Better than okay." Because what she'd said in the school newspaper interview, what she'd only wished for, would come true.

My family lost everything, but we still have each other.

Truth and Beauty, Part 3

The next morning in ELA, when Amber opened her journal, she saw the word she'd written the day she came back to school. Today, it felt like a prophecy. Like a fortune foretold.

Kindness.

Mrs. Oluonye slowly moved around the circle of desks. Unlike so many other teachers, Mrs. Oluonye acted like there was no place she'd rather be than right here, this minute, in this classroom. You knew she wanted you to feel the same way. When she paused by Amber's desk, Amber smiled up at her.

"Thanks for all your help with the Confetti Club," Amber said.

"It's been extraordinary, not a word I use lightly." Her teacher folded her hands over the knob of her cane. She leaned closer, brow wrinkling. "Remember your promise to tell me if things feel overwhelming?"

"I remember. I'm good."

"I'm always here if you need to talk."

"Okay. Thank you."

As Mrs. O. moved along, Maxwell looked at Amber and curled his lip.

"Butt kisser," he whispered.

Mei was having a sleepover after the homecoming game, and rumor was Tyler was having one, too. Mei and Tyler lived only a block apart, so who knew what might happen? Amber wondered if Lucas went to sleepovers. At lunch, Kelly B. pointed a celery stick at her.

"What are you wearing to the game?"

"Mariah's picking my outfit."

An approving nod. "You'll look great."

That afternoon, when Mom picked Amber up, she said she was worried about Gage. He'd stayed home sick from school. She'd gone over to pick him up from Dad's apartment.

Gage was pacing around Aunt Nor's family room. He looked pale and sweaty, like he was sick to his stomach, though the scraped-clean plate and empty glass on the coffee table said otherwise. Clancy jumped onto the couch and catapulted onto his back. Pretending he was getting strangled, he choked out, "Fresh air. I need fresh air."

Homer, who was infinitely cuter than he was smart, did know when a walk was about to happen. He raced out of the room and came back with his leash in his mouth. They'd only walked half a block when he zeroed in on his favorite tree-lawn-dumping spot. Gage gawked as Amber wielded the poop scoop.

"I walk him every day," she explained. "And he always saves his business for me."

"Really special," he said.

"You would not believe the things he poops out. His digestive system is a wonder of nature."

They passed a house with a colossal inflatable turkey on the front lawn. Clancy stood on tiptoe to give its beak a pat.

"Are you worrying about Friday night?" Amber asked. "I know Dad's forcing you to make a speech. Do you want any help?"

"Yeah. Make the speech for me."

"Ha ha." They walked a little farther before she said, "Speaking of Dad? You know he came to the election watch party, right? Mom was really happy to see him. They're being nicer to each other—you must've noticed. Really, who knows? On Friday night, when we get the money—"

"Where'd you get that jacket?" he interrupted. "You look like a walking doubloon."

"Thanks. That's just what I was going for."

Hurt, she let Homer pull her ahead, across the street and through the park gates. Clancy skipped ahead on the gravel path, past empty flower beds and the mermaid fountain, shut off for the season. Homer lost his mind over all the squirrels, and finally Amber collapsed on a bench. Gage, frowning at his phone, sat beside her.

"Push me!" commanded Clancy as she hopped onto a swing. "Push me, big bro!"

Gage threw a longing look at the basketball court, where some boys were laughing and trash-talking as they passed the ball around, but he trudged to the swings. When his phone, left on the bench, got a text, Amber picked it up.

Miss u every minute

The text disappeared, but not before Amber saw who'd sent it. She wrapped Homer's leash around the bench and ordered him to sit. Gage was pushing Clancy so high she was screaming in delight or terror or maybe both. Amber waved the phone as she danced toward them.

"I know something you don't know," she sang. "Guess who just texted you?" When he reached for the phone, she swung it away, but he managed to pry it from her fingers. Amber waited for him to explode with joy, but instead he spun on her, furious.

"Why are you reading my messages?"

"I'm not! Or I am but so what? Aren't you happy?" She threw her arms wide. "Ceecee wants to get back together!"

"Who's Ceecee?" Clancy asked.

"Nobody!" they yelled together, then Gage turned on Amber again. "You don't know anything about anything, okay?"

She stepped back, bewildered and angry. "Why are you being mean to me?"

"Me?" He gave Clancy's swing a shove. "I'm not the one snooping around." Another shove. "I'm not the one getting my hopes up that Mom and Dad will get back together and everything will be rainbows and unicorns." Shove. "I'm not—"

"Stop! Just stop! Why can't you believe things will be okay?"

Over on the basketball court, somebody sank a shot and shouts rang out. Gage gave Clancy another push, then stepped away, arms limp at his side. So many times, Amber had watched him cave when Dad picked on him. She'd wished Gage would stand up for himself, quit being so easy to bulldoze. Now she wished he'd stand up to her!

"Gager. Say something please."

Instead he shambled back to the bench.

"Push me!" Clancy's whine could pierce steel. Amber longed to clobber her, but instead she channeled her frustration into pushing her sister hard. Gage began typing on his phone. Sending Ceecee a message, probably. But her own phone, tucked in her jacket pocket, vibrated. She fumbled it out. Gage? Why was he texting her from a few feet away?

That night we didn't just walk around we snuck into the basement

Amber's head snapped up. Her brother was still typing.

It was just 1 cigarette & we shared it, not even the whole thing, then I put it out

Amber stopped breathing. More bubbles rose.

thought I did anyway

She stumbled back from the swing, her vision going fuzzy. Their cluttered, junky basement, the corner by the laundry chute. The bags of old curtains and bundled magazines. The vintage silver Christmas tree. She saw him and Ceecee tiptoeing down there, cuddling on the beat-up love seat, whispering in the dark, maybe kissing. Ceecee took out a cigarette and lit it, and Gage took a puff or two because he loved her and he wanted her to love him. Amber saw them tussling and play-fighting the way they had outside the Convenient Mart. Gage tossed the cigarette, but then they had to hurry if she was going to catch the bus...

"Push me!" cried Clancy the Tyrant.

On the bench, Gage sat with his head down, the last of the day's sun pressing on his bent shoulders. Over the last days he'd told her that he had a secret girlfriend, that he'd been out with her the night of the fire. In drips and drops, he'd leaked out the truth of what had happened, but he'd held back the biggest thing, the most important thing, the thing that changed it all.

Gage had started the fire. The fire that destroyed their home and could have killed her.

Clancy jumped off the swing. She hit the ground on all fours, whimpered, then popped up and ran to the bench. The swing arced back and whacked Amber's legs.

The fire that could have killed her, except he'd saved her life.

"It's okay," Clancy was telling Gage, patting his head. "Don't be sad, big bro."

A moment ago Gage had been the bravest person in the world, but now? Now Amber wasn't sure who he was. The swing bumped her again and this time she caught it, wrapping her fingers around the cold metal chains. He was still a hero, nothing could change that. Could it? But he'd started the fire, then lied about it. Did that make him a criminal? You couldn't be both a hero and a criminal, could you?

What would people think when they found out? What would they say?

Questions, more questions, whispered inside her. The Price of Kindness had raised so much money. It had become a huge, important thing. Like, The Thing. Selena, Mariah, Kelly B. and her friends—what would they do if they found out? Lucas—would he even still like her?

Amber's mind flew to the first page in her journal, where she'd written that single word: *Kindness*.

Her family didn't deserve it anymore.

Their disaster was their own fault.

The whispers grew stronger and louder till they became shouts. Mom's heart would break. And Dad. When Dad discovered the truth, there was no telling what he'd do.

"Amber!" Clancy called. "Gage is crying."

Their little sister looked scared. Amber hurried to the bench.

"I'm not crying, Clance." Gage swiped his eyes with his sleeve. "I'm just allergic to you."

Homer was whining, trying to lick Gage. "Take Homer for a little walk." Amber untied the leash. Clancy shook her head. "I'll let you play with my phone," Amber said.

"Deal."

Gage waited till Clancy was out of earshot. He peeled a splinter off the wooden bench.

"I lied about Ceecee moving away. There's no rich aunt. She's in foster care on the west side."

"That's awful."

"Her father's not in the picture and her mother is messed

up. She's trying to get Ceecee back, but every time it looks like that'll happen, something goes wrong. If she gets mixed up in this, it'll be bad." He jabbed the sliver of wood against his jeans. "I thought if I said she'd left town, it'd somehow protect her. Anyway, we both smoked the cigarette. And I'm the one who tossed it."

Ceecee with her small, anxious face, her sad, beautiful drawings. Amber felt her heart begin to stretch, but she made it stop. She snapped it back in place. It wasn't fair for Gage to take all the blame by himself! If Ceecee really loved him...

But maybe he was right. What good would it do to bring Ceecee into this? It wouldn't change anything, and it sounded like her life was already terrible. No wonder her drawings turned your heart upside down.

Gage was trying to save Ceecee, just as he'd saved Amber.

Across the grass, Clancy was pocketing acorns while Homer rolled in a pile of rotting leaves. Gage kept jabbing himself with the splinter.

"I should've told the truth right away," he said. "But I wanted to protect her and... That's not the only reason. It's like you said at Koko's, about the photos from the party. The story starts taking over, pushing out what really happened. People kept calling me a hero and before I knew what was happening, it got too hard to stop them. I almost believed it myself."

"Why didn't you tell me?"

"Why? Why lay this mess on you?"

"Because!" She took the splinter from him and flung it away. "You're my brother. It's my mess, too."

His eyes met hers and he winced. "I never wanted you to look at me like you are right now."

Amber pressed her cold hands to her hot cheeks, ashamed. Gage needed her. Ceecee might miss him, she might even love him, but he wouldn't let her help him.

Gage had no one except Amber now.

"You don't know what it's been like," he said. "Every time somebody shakes my hand, I want to run. Instead I have to smile and say thanks, and the whole time I'm thinking, if they only knew. I lie awake at night thinking, Okay. Tomorrow I'll tell Dad. No matter what happens, I don't care. I can't keep living this lie. Then it's morning and he's making me breakfast, nagging me to get my protein, saying he's working the late shift but he trusts me to stay in, do my homework, and no way I can tell him the truth. Another day goes by."

Clancy and Homer were trotting back. The dog, a big stick in his jaws, looked ridiculously proud.

"I won't tell," Amber said quietly. "You know that, right?"

"I'm not asking you to do that."

"You don't have to ask!"

Clancy squeezed onto the bench between them, a little book between two big bookends. Homer threw himself down and chomped his stick. By now the basketball kids were gone and a pale slice of moon hung in the sky. A squirrel went up on two legs to look at them, as if wondering why they didn't go home.

But the three of them kept sitting there. It was how they used to sit on the living room couch, sometimes doing things separately but sometimes watching a movie, playing a video game, passing a bag of chips back and forth. When Clancy was learning her letters, Gage helped her, and when Amber was trying to figure out a new app, he helped her, too. He let Clancy paint his toenails and taught her how to fake burp. Once Amber fell asleep during a movie and woke up to find him carefully pulling off her shoes.

This was how they were meant to be. This was how they *would* be, if no one ever found out the truth about the fire. They'd have the money from the fundraiser, and Mom and Dad would get back together. At school, she wouldn't be the old invisible Amber Price but the girl whose brother was a hero, whose family was so close, the girl they'd showered with kindness.

Mrs. Oluonye's quote was all wrong. Truth was not beauty. It was ugly. Ugly enough to ruin your whole world.

"Gage, they still don't have any actual proof. They could still let it all go."

"Let what go?" Clancy asked.

"Nothing!" Amber and Gage cried together. Amber quickly deleted the texts they'd just sent, then handed the phone to Clancy. Lowering her voice, she said, "If we just wait, maybe they'll close the investigation."

Gage stared at her across the top of Clancy's head. "What are you saying?"

"Just... it was an accident. You didn't do anything wrong. I mean, nothing more wrong than me not putting the smoke detector battery back or getting trapped in your room so you had to—"

"Stop." Gage stood up. "You know this is different."

They walked back, past the shut-down mermaid fountain, through the gates and across the street. When they got to the blow-up turkey, Clancy ran across the grass to take a photo with Amber's phone. Amber pushed her hands deep into her golden pockets.

"We don't have to tell. If we stick together, we can keep this our secret."

There. She'd said it.

He'd thought the same thing, she could tell. But he shook his head.

"I can't. How am I supposed to stand in front of that crowd and make a speech? How am I supposed to take all that money? I can't do it."

She hugged herself against the cold. The fundraiser was happening because of her. She'd talked—or maybe tricked, but anyway—Gage into it. She'd gotten him to convince Dad. And it was still a good thing. Wasn't it? The best thing for them all? It was. It had to be.

"I'll be there. I'll help you. People don't need to know, Gage. They—they don't even want to know."

"Maybe." He ran his hand up over the back of his head. "It's true, if I just keep quiet, everybody will be happy. Plus, getting the money is probably my one chance to make it up to you and Mom and Dad for what I did." His hair stood on end. His lower lip twitched. "I don't know, though. What if I blow it?"

"You won't." And then she promised it again. "I'll be there."

On the Verge

Thursday.

In ELA, it was grammar and punctuation day. Mrs. Oluonye's champion of the prepositional phrase, lover of colons and semicolons, tried her best to make the lesson entertaining. Today she read from a book called *Eats, Shoots & Leaves*, giving funny examples of how commas can change a sentence's meaning.

"Eats poop and heaves," Maxwell said. Which got him some laughs, as well as a time-out in the hallway.

Kelly B. held her nose as he sauntered past her on his way out, and Amber saw Maxwell's face crumple for an instant. Could he possibly like Kelly? That would be a crush so impossible, he might as well be in love with the moon.

Her heart twisted. Like me, she thought, back when I could only dream that Lucas might like me.

Now she remembered what Lucas had said about Maxwell's brother going to juvie. A brother in trouble with the law. Her heart twisted again, this time so tight that she couldn't breathe.

• • •

At their lockers before lunch, Lottie told Amber that her parents were getting a babysitter for James so they could come to the homecoming game.

"Isla actually said I could sit by her, not *with* her since she'll be in the band section with the other majorettes, but in her vicinity. By Her Royal Majesty's standards, this is the height of generosity. Of course I told her I'd be sitting with my own friends." Lottie fingered her chin, which despite all her efforts had broken out again.

"Well." Amber paused. "Selena says there's going to be a stage where my family's supposed to sit."

"Oh. Sure. I should have figured that."

"Maybe you can sit with Mariah?"

Before, that wouldn't even have been a question. Suddenly, Amber missed Lottie so much, she couldn't stand it.

"Don't practice viola today," she blurted. "Come eat lunch with me! We won't sit with Kelly B. We can sit at our old table."

Lottie hesitated, and now Amber bit her tongue, suddenly afraid Lottie would say okay. How could she spend an entire lunch period without telling Lottie the truth about Gage? She felt the words scrabbling their claws inside her, demanding to be let out. How had Gage managed to keep things to himself so long? Even small secrets tried to get out, but this one? It gnawed. It howled. Lottie slowly spun her locker combination.

"Mr. Halliday is going to work with me on some fingerings," she said then. Translation: *Amber, I know where you really want to sit at lunch.*

Friday.

Amber woke before dawn to discover only Clancy on the futon. Slipping downstairs, she found Mom curled up in a corner of the family room couch, the light from her laptop softly glowing.

"Sweetie," she said, looking up. "What are you doing awake?"

"I can't sleep."

Mom patted the couch beside her. When Amber nestled close, she turned the screen so Amber could see a design of yellow flowering vines spelled out *La Tige* on a deep purple background.

"It's French for *The Stem*. I'm designing a new logo for a florist shop. On spec. That means they won't pay me unless they like it."

"They'll like it, Mom."

"I had some other ideas, too."

She showed Amber more versions, and they discussed

the pros and cons of each. Homer came to investigate what these humans were doing up so early, and when he realized it didn't involve food, he sighed, circled three times, and lay down on the rug at their feet. Outside the sliding glass doors, the dark sky was slowly turning pearly gray. Mom set her laptop aside and pulled the warty beige afghan over them both.

"It's been so hard, sweetie. Maybe I shouldn't tell you this, but for a while, I couldn't figure out how—if—I'd handle what happened. It felt like everything we'd ever had was lost, and how could we possibly start all over?" She stroked Amber's hair. "But this morning when I woke up, I felt truly hopeful for the first time." She kissed the top of Amber's head. "We're on the verge of something new. I can feel it."

Kelly B. and her crew's *Price of Kindness* shirts were pink with fuchsia lettering, and the O was a heart. Mariah and the soccer girls had black-and-white shirts, with a red soccer ball for the O.

"I guess I didn't get the memo," Lottie said. She was wearing her gray Mathlete tee, which read *We Will Kick Your Asymptote.*

At the end of the day, Principal Stefanski came on the PA to remind everyone about tonight. Cougar roars rocked the building. When the bell rang and people surged into the halls, Lucas caught up with Amber.

"Hey, are you going to Mei's sleepover?"

"I'm not sure."

"Because if you're not I was thinking maybe we could hang out. Maybe watch a movie or something at my house? I know your family might have plans, but I was hoping anyway."

He was hoping.

"Can I text you?"

They ducked around the corner and quickly traded phones, tapping in their numbers.

Had Lucas just asked her out?

He had, hadn't he?

Off the Hook

Amber was ready ahead of time. Way ahead. She wore the black jeans and violet sweater Mariah had given her, even though she had to roll the bottoms of the jeans up three times. She tried putting her hair up, back, and sideways, but finally just left it brushed out over her shoulders. She hated to ruin it all with her bad high-tops, so she put on the boots even though they were toe torture.

Too nervous to sit down, she paced the upstairs hallway, boot heels loud on the wood floor, hushed on the woven rug. Loud, hushed, loud, hushed. Bert and Ernie were bent over the chessboard and she stopped in their doorway to watch. Bert reached for a pawn. Amber had watched them so often, she found herself whispering, "Maybe not?"

Her cousins looked up in surprise. Then Bert gave a soft *hmmm*. She tapped her chin and picked up her knight instead.

Downstairs, Clancy, wearing her musk ox horns, was watching out for Dad's car. The plan was to meet here, then drive to the high school together in time for the halftime ceremony. Clancy commented on every vehicle that went by.

"Not Dad. Not Dad. Still not Dad."

"Clance, it's not time yet."

"Dad will be early."

Aunt Nor's family was going out to eat, then to the high school. Once they left, the house was unnaturally quiet. Clancy took up her vigil at the window again, and this time Homer kept her company.

"Not Dad. Not Dad. Not...Dad! He's here!" When she pulled open the front door, Homer shot out to discharge three slobbery tennis balls at their father's feet. Amber hauled the dog inside and gave him a biscuit from the bowl Aunt Nor kept on the hall table.

"You know you're reinforcing his bad behavior," Dad said.

"Hi, Dad," Amber said.

He wore a suit and a tie. She hadn't seen him so dressed up since—she couldn't remember when. Plus, he'd gotten a killer haircut. Killer, as in the barber had massacred his head. Dad was as close to bald as a not-bald man could be. Had he even gotten his eyebrows trimmed? He looked handsome but also nervous. He pulled out a handkerchief (one of his real handkerchiefs) and mopped his brow.

Gage wore khakis and a long-sleeved collared shirt. Without a hoodie, he looked scrawny. Clancy threw her arms around him.

"Ow," he yelped. "What's with the horns?"

"I'm a musk ox. I survived the Ice Age."

"You're not wearing that helmet to the ceremony," Dad said.

"I know that. Do you realize I'm practically seven years old?"

"Excuse me." Dad smiled.

"Mom's almost ready," Amber said, hoping it was true. "Let's sit in the family room."

Dad perched on the edge of the couch. He ran a finger around the inside of his collar. "You've got your speech, right?" he asked Gage.

From the way Gage dragged an index card from his pocket, Amber could tell Dad had already asked him this several hundred times. Gage set the card on the arm of the couch. He was moving carefully, as if every tiny motion took consideration. In the end, he hadn't let Amber help him with the speech. Who knew what it said? She slid her pendant back and forth on its chain, longing to catch his eye, but he was busy studying the ceiling.

"It's natural to be anxious, buddy," Dad said. "What you do is, use the adrenaline to focus your concentration. You just—what am I saying?" He blew a breath. "I can't wait to get this over with either. Listen. You're going to have the world's friendliest audience. You can read them the grocery list and they'll be happy."

Amber tried to get a look at the index card. Gage's

handwriting was always terrible, but what she saw looked like hieroglyphics. No way she could read it.

"Sorry!" Mom rushed into the room wearing the new dress and tights she'd bought. Her hair was already slipping free of its ponytail, but her eyes were as starry as her twinkly earrings. Amber was sure she'd never looked more beautiful.

When Dad pecked her on the cheek, Mom pecked him back. Amber darted a look at Gage. *See? I told you they're getting close again!* But her brother was still staring at the ceiling like he was responsible for holding it up.

"How are you doing, sweetie?" Mom asked him.

"Great. Except for wanting to throw up." He gave her a crooked smile. "Just kidding, Mom."

She insisted on getting him a glass of water, which he insisted on not drinking. Dad cleared his throat.

"Now that we're all together, I have some news," he said. "This afternoon I got a call from Jeremy Thompkins at Allied Insurance."

Amber's heart escaped her chest and flew around the room.

"It turns out Thompkins has a nephew at the high school. He's a football player. Thompkins knew all about tonight. Anyway." Dad plucked at the crease in his pants. "They're ready to close the case."

Amber's heart slammed back into place. Gage jumped like his own heart had done the same thing.

"Who's Jeremy Thompkins?" Clancy demanded, but everyone ignored her.

"That's good," Mom said. "It's good, isn't it?"

"Depends how you look at it," Dad said. "They'll only pay a fraction of what the house was worth. They're citing negligence, since the basement was a fire hazard." He pounded his fist on his knee. "I can't believe I didn't get that mess cleaned out. It was on my list, but something else was always coming up, getting in the way. If only—"

"Dad," Amber said. "It's not your fault!"

He shook his head. His shoulders sagged. Amber didn't dare look at her brother.

"Gus, what's done is done. We need to move on." Mom took his chin and gently turned his face toward hers. "Tonight's our chance to do that. Our community's done a wonderful, generous thing for us. Our son is a hero. What more do we need?"

When Mom touched her forehead to Dad's, Amber watched something in him surrender. He slowly stood, held out a hand, and pulled Gage to his feet.

"Come on, bud," Dad said. "Let's get this dog-and-pony show over with!"

"Don't put it like that!" Mom protested, but Amber saw, with a tingle of hope, that she and Dad were holding hands.

Spotlight

The high school parking lot was full. Dad circled it twice, then let them out and drove off to find a spot on the street. The football field was lit up brighter than day, and the stands were packed. Banners proclaimed WELCOME HOME, COUGARS! A loudspeaker announced a play on the field, and trumpets blared.

"Charge!" yelled the crowd.

Amber was dying to speak to Gage alone. *See?* she'd say. *You're off the hook! It's all good!*

But it was so loud, and the crowd was so dense they had to thread their way single file around the edge of the field. The air smelled of hot dogs and popcorn, and little kids darted in and out of the shadows, playing tag beneath the bleachers. High school kids, middle school kids, adults, people so old they must have been students here at the dawn of time. Classmates, neighbors, strangers, all in high spirits. There was Mr. Taherian with his rosy-faced wife and their children, and was that really Mr. Getty, wearing a long overcoat that made him look like a spy? Aunt Nor and Uncle Neither called to them as the little twins furiously dueled with cougar pennants. Mariah and the soccer girls went wild when they saw Amber, and when the same thing happened as they passed Kelly B. and her crew, Mom gave her a surprised and pleased look.

"So many friends, sweetie!"

"You're utterly popular," Clancy said. "Just like me."

Amber didn't see Lottie, but magically, miraculously, she spotted Lucas high up in the stands. He sat with a bunch of other boys including—who'd have predicted it—Maxwell. The night was clear and cold, but all at once Amber felt too warm and tugged on her golden jacket's zipper.

"Gaaaaage!" yelled some girls. "Look this way, Gage Price!"

Phones went up, pictures snapped. Two girls ran over, and he had to stop so they could take selfies with him.

"They want to marry you," Clancy said.

The loudspeaker boomed. "And that's the end of the first half!" A whistle blew and the players trotted off the field. "Folks, you are in for a treat! Let's give it up for the award-winning Cougar marching band and their spectacular half-time show!"

Isla led the way onto the field, baton held high, knees lifting till they practically touched her nose. The other majorettes followed and then the marching band, drums rolling, brass clamoring, the kind of music that takes over the world. Clancy marched in place, tossing an invisible baton. Dad, who'd finally found a parking spot, caught up with them, his face flushed.

"Wow." He wiped his brow. "This is really something."

A platform with chairs and a mic was set up on the edge of the field. Mr. Monaghan was there and when he spied their family, he gestured for them to step up. Gage lagged behind, looking like he might, after all, barf. Maybe the news hadn't sunk in yet. Maybe he still couldn't process that it was all going to work out. Amber waited for him to catch up, then stood on tiptoe and put her lips to his ear, the only way he could hear her over the noise.

"The case is closed!"

He shrugged her off. A bad taste rose in the back of her mouth. She swallowed it down and tried again.

"Everything's going to be—"

"I forgot my speech at Aunt Nor's."

"Oh, is that all? I thought—" What? What did she think? Something much worse. But no. It was just his speech. That was all.

"What's the matter?" Mom turned around.

"Nothing," Amber said. "I mean, well, except Gage left his speech at Aunt Nor's."

"Are you kidding me?" Dad thundered.

They stood in a family knot, trying to hear one another

over the band and the crowd. Mom said it didn't matter, Gage could just say thank you, but Dad said not with all these people expecting more.

"Take a minute," he told Gage. "Gather your thoughts. You can still do this."

"I don't think so," Gage said.

"Just speak from your heart," Mom said. "Keep it simple and true."

"Mom's right. You got this, Gage Price." Dad clapped him on the back as the crowd gave a roar. Out on the field, the band stood in a formation, and though it was impossible, from where she was, to read the words, Amber could guess.

The B is really tricky, Lottie had said, *but they're going to spell out* BE KIND.

Gage's eyes darted from the crowd to the microphone and back. Amber shut her eyes and tried to send him a mental message.

Our secret won't hurt anyone, as long we keep it. And I will, forever and ever.

But the message wouldn't send. She could feel it trapped and buzzing inside her own brain.

"Thank you, Cougar marching band!" the announcer said as Isla and her baton led the band off the field. "In a few moments, we'll begin tonight's very special program!"

"Here we go," Dad said.

They stepped onto the platform where a woman who introduced herself as Shontel Bibb, the newly elected mayor, shook their hands, warmly thanking Mom for her work on the campaign. Selena, in her usual jeans, and Justin, wearing a three-piece suit and bow tie, were there, too. The mega-bright lights made everyone look a little vampirish.

The superintendent of schools, a short, stocky man, stepped up and tapped the mic, which squealed the way school mics always did, making people clap their hands over their ears. When he had it adjusted, he extended a hearty welcome to Cougars of all ages and gave a short speech. Shontel Bibb said a new lines about how proud she was to serve this generous community. Next came Mr. Monaghan, wearing a Tweety Bird tie. He launched into an endless speech full of quotes about leadership, teamwork, and who knew what else. As he droned on, it came to Amber how much these grown-ups were enjoying standing in the spotlight, courtesy of Gage. Because of him, they got a chance to shine, too.

She looked at Dad, his chin up, shoulders back. He hadn't wanted this fundraiser, but now he was basking in Gage's glow, too.

Gage was here for Dad. He was here for Mom. He was here for her. He was here for their family, to make up for what he'd done, and for the community, to give them the hero they wanted to believe in.

There was only one person Gage *wasn't* here for.

Himself.

It was Mrs. Stefanski's turn next, but just as she took the mic, a child yelled out from the stands.

"Hi, Clancy!"

Clancy jumped off her chair and waved. "Hi, Eva!" she yelled back.

When the crowd cheered, Mrs. Stefanski laughed.

"Clancy and Eva, you're right! Time to turn this program over to the students who made it possible. It's my great pleasure to introduce Selena Hernandez and Justin Cotton, representatives of Cloverville Middle's Confetti Club, who will now make a very important presentation."

Selena and Justin stepped up. Justin lowered the mic stand and straightened his bow tie. "'Spread kindness like confetti!' That is our motto." He paused as the crowd applauded. "In case you aren't sure what kindness is, here is the dictionary definition. 'Kindness is the quality of being friendly, generous, and considerate.' This sounds good, but it's not always easy. First, it can be hard to be a friend to someone you don't know or someone who isn't like you. Second, the sad fact is, it's easier to be selfish than generous. And third, consider considerate. That means thinking others are as important as you are."

Justin didn't have any notes. He must have memorized

his speech. Selena glanced back at Amber and grinned. *Can you believe what a good job the little guy's doing?*

"So, kindness can be a real challenge. Yet, science has proven that animals of different species look out for each other. Even trees share knowledge and communicate through their root systems. So, shouldn't humankind be both human and kind?"

Amber felt the goodwill rolling toward them, wrapping her and her family in an enormous, communal hug. When she glanced sideways, she saw tears pooling in Mom's eyes, Dad reaching for her hand. She told herself it was the harsh lights that made Gage look like all the blood had drained out of him.

"And so without further ado." Justin turned. "Gage Price, could you please step forward?"

Up in the bleachers, the band did a drumroll. Gage slid to the edge of his chair, where he froze.

"Go get 'em, bud," Dad said.

"You'll do fine, sweetie," Mom said.

When Clancy jumped out of her chair and pulled him to his feet, the crowd ate it up. They were already clapping as Gage stepped to the mic, which Selena was adjusting. By now Amber's heart was beating as loud as that drum, too loud to be sure what Selena said. And then, all at once, the crowd grew quiet.

It was Gage's turn.

"This is—this is—" He shook his head. He tried again. "I want—I can't."

A hush fell. He stepped away from the mic, then suddenly lunged back toward it.

"I'm really sorry," he blurted, then jumped down from the platform and raced away.

Puzzled laughter from the stands. Was this a joke? What was happening? Selena turned a confused and anxious face to Amber.

"Some hero!" a voice called from high in the bleachers. It sounded like Maxwell. "He can't even say thank you?"

"Quiet!" yelled someone else. "Give the kid a break!"

Mom stumbled to her feet. For a moment she, too, stood frozen in the lights.

"Sit down," Dad said out of the corner of his mouth. "Don't make this worse."

Instead, Mom clattered down the platform steps and hurried after Gage.

Amber's heart flew after them. But all the rest of her stayed glued to her seat.

The stands were starting to buzz. Dad got up, straightened his tie, and walked to the mic. He coughed into his elbow. Then coughed again.

"I'm Gus Price and I apologize for my son. He, uh, he

was pretty nervous about this. Go figure. He was brave enough to rush into a burning building, but too scared to give a speech."

There was laughter, a spatter of applause, and then Justin stepped forward, holding up a large facsimile of a check.

"Mr. Price, on behalf of the Confetti Club of Cloverville Middle School, I now present your family with this check. It's not a real check, it's just for show. But you really will get all that money!"

"Thank you for your generosity to our family." Dad choked up. "We will never forget this."

Applause, a trumpet fanfare. The loudspeaker announced that this was the end of halftime, and the third quarter would begin in a few minutes.

Without a word, Dad stepped down and headed across the field, avoiding the stands. Somehow Amber, legs weak and shaking, heart racing, managed to grab Clancy's hand and follow.

End of Story

They caught up with Mom and Gage half a block away.

"Wait here," Dad ordered. "I'll get the car."

You could still hear the game from where they stood—the muffled voice of the announcer, the muted blare of brass. Amber remembered Selena's confused face, heard Maxwell's stupid voice. She imagined everyone asking each other, *What just happened?* Gage hadn't even said thank you. Instead, he'd told everyone he was sorry.

She looked at her brother, whose arms hung at his side like he'd finally set down something heavy. Dad drove up and they all got in.

"Well," Mom said. "That didn't exactly go as planned."

"Best-laid plans." Dad shook his head. "It's a crying shame you forgot to bring the speech. But you're not the first person who ever caved under pressure. That was some crowd!"

"You gave an utterly perfect speech, Daddy," Clancy said.

Dad gave a little snort, but Amber could tell he was pleased.

She stole a glance at her phone. A dozen texts, including one from Lucas. **Where r u?**

What should she tell people? She struggled to decide. Gage getting the jitters—everyone would understand that. She could say he'd written a wonderful speech but forgotten it, then gotten paralyzed by stage fright. Stage fright so bad he was afraid he'd puke. Should she say that? It would be sort of true—not all the way true, but true enough.

This was still her story to tell. Wasn't it?

When they got to Dad's apartment, he and Clancy went into the kitchen while Mom and Amber sat on the ugly brown sofa and Gage took one of the straight-backed, instrument-of-torture chairs.

"Sit with us," Mom told him, scooching over, but he didn't move.

Amber pinched the amber pendant, slid it back and forth on the chain.

"Gage?" she said, voice low. "The speech doesn't matter. Everything will still be okay."

When he looked up at her, her skin suddenly grew too tight. She didn't need to close her eyes, didn't need to stick her fingers in her ears. She could read her brother's thoughts as clearly as if they were printed on his forehead.

"Don't," she said. "Please don't ruin everything."

"Careful!" Mom cried as Clancy tottered across the

room carrying a bakery cake. Mom gave Dad a delighted look. "Augustus Price, as long as I've known you, I can't remember you ever buying a cake!"

"That can't be true," he said, setting down plates and forks. He loosened his tie. "Though it might be."

"Come on, sweetie," Mom told Gage. "Shake off those blues. You cut the first piece." When Gage didn't move, Amber grabbed the knife.

"I'll do it!" She cut an enormous slice and held it out to her brother, who shook his head.

"Sorry, Amboo," he said. "I can't."

"Can't eat cake?" Mom said. "Is this the real Gage Price?" She put a hand on his knee. "Dad's right. By tomorrow no one will care that you fumbled the speech. Tomorrow you'll—"

"I mean I can't keep doing this," Gage said.

Amber still held out the plate. She needed him to take the cake. She needed him to eat it, to swallow it down. Swallow his words down.

The night of the fire, she hadn't saved anything. Not even herself. Gage had done that.

Now she needed to save him.

"Gage," she whispered. "Think what you're doing!"

Dad had pulled off his tie and was just beginning to look relaxed.

"Think about what?" he said. "What's going on now?"

Gage took the plate from Amber and set it down. His face was apologetic. And scared. But most of all it was determined. "It's the right thing," he told her. "I have to do this."

"Do what?" Dad demanded.

Gage drew a ragged breath. "The fire was my fault," he said.

Amber fell back against the couch. All the air emptied out of her. It was no use, it was all over. Her brother's voice grew stronger as he described that night. He held his head up and told the whole story, starting with lying about where he was going, then meeting up with Ceecee, the cigarette, coming back to find the house in flames. He spoke without pausing or stumbling, as different as could be from the boy who'd stood on the platform less than an hour ago. It was like he was breathing out the fire's thick, gritty smoke all over again, clearing his heart and lungs once and for all. Their parents listened in shocked silence.

"I'm sorry," Gage said at last. "I know you're ashamed."

"Ashamed?" Dad was on his feet. He was yanking Gage out of the chair. "Ashamed?"

"Gus!" Mom cried. "Don't!"

Dad gripped Gage's shoulders and shook him so hard his head snapped back. Gage made a small choking sound, and then he began to cry.

"Stop!" Mom pushed her way between them. "Gus, stop it right now!"

Dad stepped back. Strict as he was, Dad rarely yelled and he never hurt them. Now he looked like he hardly knew what he was doing. He rocked back on his heels.

"You've been lying to us all this time? How could you do that?"

"I don't know. I was scared."

Dad folded his arms tight, like he was trying to keep from grabbing Gage again. Clancy plastered herself against Amber.

"Everything happened so fast." Gage wiped his eyes. "The hero stuff... it got out of control. It started taking over and I didn't know how to stop it."

"You mean you didn't want to," Dad said.

"Okay," Gage said miserably. "That too."

"I can't believe you didn't tell us right away, that night."

"Gus, are you forgetting? He was badly hurt." Mom tried to put an arm around Gage but he shook her off.

"Don't make excuses for me, Mom. I could've told, but I was scared to let everyone down." He looked straight at Dad. "Especially you."

Dad flinched, then looked away.

"You shouldn't have been afraid to tell us, Gage," Mom said. "That's on us."

"Are you defending what he did?" Dad cried. "Is that what I'm hearing?"

"Why do you put everything in those terms?" Mom spun on him, her face a blur of tears and fury. "As if there's always a clear wrong and right! Can't you see how much pain Gage is in? Where's your heart, Gus?"

Dad pressed a hand to his chest, as if checking there still was an organ in there. For a moment, he looked as pained and sorry as Gage.

"There's truth and there are lies," he said through his teeth. "Some people value the difference."

"I screwed up." Gage drew a shuddery breath. "I screwed up. I'm sorry."

"Too late for that," Dad said. "You made fools of us in front of the whole town and that's the least of it. We need to report this. The police need to know."

"Police!" Amber was stunned. "Dad, no!" Her father shot her a look.

"You didn't know about this, did you?" he said.

"Leave her out of this!" Gage cried, but Dad ignored him.

"Amber, answer me. Did you know?"

His eyes pinned her. She shrank back against the couch. So this was what it was like! Amber never got in trouble, not big, enormous trouble like this, and it came to her now that, as much as she hated how Dad picked on Gage, it had made her life easier. Dad never got as angry at her, never found as much fault with her. This was what Gage went through.

And now her brother was trying to save her from it.

"Amber." Dad's voice was taut as wire. "I'm waiting."

She looked at her big brother and understood that if she said no, she hadn't known, she was as surprised and shocked as Dad was—if she lied, Gage would have her back. Gage stood up for people he loved.

Could she ever be as brave as he was?

"I knew." She wished her voice was stronger. "I knew."

Like a light had suddenly zapped his eyes, a light so bright it blinded him—that was how Dad looked. He blinked and turned away, but not before Amber saw his face collapse on itself like it did that day he drove her home from the hospital, when he told her that if he'd been there, the fire never would have happened. His world had gotten away from him and he didn't know how to get it back.

"I'm sorry, too." Amber willed her voice not to tremble, but it did, big-time. "I told Gage to lie. Even when I knew how bad he was hurting, I wanted him to lie."

And I still wish he did.

Aunt Nor claimed Amber was the family anchor, but she was wrong. Amber was the iceberg, slicing the ship in half, sinking it to the bottom of the sea.

Their strict father, their rule-abiding, their always-had-the-answer father, sat down. They all watched as he took a bite of the cake Amber had cut for Gage. Another bite. He kept eating until the big slice was gone, then set the plate back down. He wiped his lips with a napkin.

"Gus," Mom said at last. "We need to talk. We need to figure this out together."

Dad put down the napkin. "What's there to figure out?"

"I know you're hurt but—"

"I'm not hurt. I'm disgusted."

"Fine. Shut us out. Go ahead!"

"Stop stop stop!" Clancy clapped her hands over her ears. "Stop stop I hate you stop!" Amber pulled her sister close. As if there was any protecting her. "I want to go home," Clancy sobbed.

As if they still had one.

Waiting

Mom refused to let Dad drive them back to Aunt Nor's. She called a car and the four of them went outside to wait for it. Amber glanced up at the lighted window of Dad's apartment. There he stood.

Still watching over them. Even though by now he knew he couldn't keep them safe.

Mom must have texted Aunt Nor, because when they got there she'd already made up the family room couch for Gage. He crawled onto it, still wearing his shirt and khakis. Mom pulled the lumpy beige afghan over him, kissed his forehead, and tiptoed out, closing the double doors behind her.

Up in the guest room, Amber checked her phone. More than a dozen new texts, but the only one she could stand to open was Lottie's.

Things ok?

She was trying to decide what to answer when her mother came in.

"Mom, what am I supposed to tell people?"

"Tell people?" Mom sounded as if the thought of others hadn't occurred to her. "Oh, sweetie, I have no idea."

A new text from Lottie popped up.

G ok? U????????

Clancy came in, smelling of toothpaste and wearing her horns. Amber was suddenly so tired, tired in a deep, drowning way, that she could hardly pull the painful boots off her feet. She curled up on the futon, her mother on one side of her, her sister on the other, her brother downstairs. All her family under the same roof again, except...

She saw her father alone in the upstairs window. Slivers of sorrow pierced her heart.

When she woke the next morning, Clancy and Mom were gone. She lay listening to the eerily quiet house. Her phone (more texts) said it was nearly noon, but she still felt exhausted. If only she could stay in bed for the rest of her life.

She rolled over, mashing her face in her pillow. Last night, last night—she couldn't stand to think of it. She really, truly couldn't. When she tried, it only came back in bits. The cheering crowd, Selena's bright smile, Dad's chest puffed with pride, Gage stumbling off the platform, the cake, Clancy wailing.

She dragged herself up and pulled on clothes. Phone in hand, she stumbled downstairs. A note on the kitchen island said that Uncle Neither had taken Bert and Ernie to a weekend chess tournament and Aunt Nor and the little twins were helping at the food pantry. Mom had taken Clancy to the movies for a treat.

The doors to the family room were still shut. When Amber peeked in, she saw her brother cocooned in the hideous afghan, a single tuft of hair poking out. It looked like he hadn't moved an inch. He probably never wanted to get up again either.

Before they left his apartment last night, Dad said he'd take Gage to the police station this afternoon. She couldn't stand to think of it.

She really truly couldn't.

Except.

Except people still didn't know the truth about the fire.

That was still their secret.

Maybe...maybe she could still save things.

Amber quietly closed the family room doors. She tapped in Dad's number.

"Lamber." He picked up right away. His voice was rough, as if he hadn't slept. "Is everyone okay? I've been trying to call your mother but she doesn't pick up."

"She and Clancy went to the movies." Amber reached for her pendant, then remembered she'd left it on the nightstand. "Dad. I'm sorry we lied."

"I know you are."

"It was a big mistake. And I'm really, really sorry. But Dad? Telling the truth now? It will make things way worse."

Why did she say that? What was she thinking? Dad and the truth—they were synonyms! He'd never, ever agree to be part of a lie. Amber leaned against the wall, then slid down to the floor. Earrings hopped into her lap. Her father said nothing. Then more nothing. She stroked the bunny's fur, braced for the lecture. When Dad finally spoke, his voice sounded full of holes.

"You really think I *want* to put your brother through this? Is that how you think of me?"

"No. I mean..." What did she mean? "I guess I'm not sure."

Quiet on the other end of the line.

"We can wait a little longer," he said at last. "Your mother's right. We have to figure this out together. We need to talk this through before we do anything."

After they said goodbye, Amber waited to feel better.

She waited and waited. But that rough weight on her chest, like she'd swallowed a piece of sidewalk or maybe a meteorite, took up too much space. It left no room for anything else.

The doorbell rang. When she opened the door, Mariah flew in.

Amber's (Almost) Third Lie

"Amber ambush!" Mariah wore her soccer uniform, her hair in a soccer-girl fishtail braid. "Since you're not answering my texts, I decided to come in person. My mom dropped me off after the game."

Amber led her to the kitchen, where Mariah gazed wide-eyed at the sink piled with pots and pans, the campaign signs leaning in a corner, Earrings crouched in his litter box. "Your aunt's house is, um, interesting." She slid onto a stool. "Okay. What in the world is going on?"

Amber grabbed a sponge and began to wipe up juice and coffee rings. It was impossible to look her best friend in the eye. She'd never lied to Mariah before. Tiny fibs, sure, but not actual, significant lies.

"The whole thing is so embarrassing." From the corner of her eye, she watched Mariah lick a finger and carefully rub a grass stain on her knee. Amber kept scrubbing the counter, both of them rubbing and scrubbing, trying to clean things up. "Poor Gage. He had such bad stage fright, I'm surprised he didn't pass out."

"Is he okay?"

"He will be, I guess."

"You know Mei. Her mother's president of the PTA. She says your father called last night and asked if it was possible to donate the money to some other cause. Mei's mom told him it wasn't a PTA thing and he needed to talk to Mrs. Oluonye but anyway." Mariah's brow puckered. "Why would he do that?"

This was news. Amber scrubbed the counter. Her brain spun. Her story needed more work.

"Who knows?" she tried. "Dad kept saying we didn't need charity. You know how he is! But I never expected that he'd—"

"That he'd change his mind like this." Mariah finished her sentence, then made an I'm-sorry face. "Mei wasn't supposed to tell anyone. But I guess she told Kelly B. and now everybody's wondering what's going on. I got so sick of the rumors. I knew you'd tell me the actual truth."

Her eyes searched Amber's face. They'd been best friends so long, and in the last weeks they'd grown even closer. Shame flooded Amber.

"I guess he doesn't think we deserve the money."

Mariah tilted her head. For a long moment, the only sound was Earrings munching his bunny hay.

"But then why did he let us do the fundraiser in the first place?" Mariah asked. "And why did he say he'd never forget it? It doesn't make sense. Plus, why wouldn't you deserve it?"

Mariah was so different from Lottie, whose face rarely

revealed the thoughts shooting across her steel-trap brain. Mariah's face showed everything. Confusion, doubt, and then hurt.

"People thought you'd be happy and grateful. They're going to be extremely upset if you turn down the money."

"I know. You don't need to tell me that."

"I don't?" The hurt in Mariah's eyes shifted into something else. "It seems like maybe I do need to tell you, though. Like maybe your family doesn't understand how much this meant to people."

Amber set down the sponge. She could continue casting her father as the bad guy. Mariah knew how unreasonable he could be. Her best friend would sympathize.

But now Amber saw Dad standing alone in his apartment window, heard him asking on the phone, *Is that what you think of me?* She saw Gage looking at her, sorry but determined. *It's the right thing. I have to do this.* All at once, she was out of stories to tell.

All at once, she was ashamed of being ashamed.

"I'm sorry," she said. "But could you please not disrespect my family?"

Mariah drew back. "I'm just telling you how this makes me feel."

"I know, but—"

"But?" For once Mariah didn't finish Amber's sentence.

"I don't know," Amber said.

"I was so happy helping the club and making a difference! It was like I was doing something *real*, something that actually mattered. Now it turns out all that kindness was for nothing?" Mariah got to her feet. Her eyes were green pools. "I think you're the one disrespecting us."

"I'm sorry," Amber whispered again.

"I don't know what's going on." Mariah waited for Amber to say something, but when Amber didn't, she moved toward the door. "When you're ready to tell me, I'll be ready to listen."

Amber heard the front door close. Somehow, she managed to climb the stairs and crawl back onto the futon. Who knew how long she lay there before Mom stuck her head in the door.

"Amber? Where's Gage?"

She sat up. "He's not here?"

"I was on the way back from the movies when Dad called to say we should talk, but when I got here, Gage was gone. He didn't leave a note." Mom poked her lip. "He didn't say anything to you?"

"No."

"He was expecting Dad to take him to the police station." Mom sank onto the futon. "Maybe he couldn't face it."

"Mom." Amber took her mother's hand. "If there's one thing we know by now, it's that Gage is brave."

"Then where is he?"

Willow Heart

Mom called his friends, but nobody had seen him. Amber didn't know Ceecee's number, not even her last name. When Mom called Dad, he came over right away and the two of them left to drive around looking.

Hours went by.

Clancy wouldn't stop asking if Gage had died.

"Don't be silly!" Amber smoothed her cowlick. "He's fine. He just needs some space, is all. He'll be back soon."

Please let that be true.

By now she'd lost count of how many times she'd texted him.

"Ice cream social!" Aunt Nor announced as she lined up cartons of ice cream and toppings on the kitchen island. While Clancy and the twins filled their bowls, she pulled Amber aside. "You're not covering up for him, are you?"

"What? No!" Did her aunt really think she'd do that?

"Okay, okay, just checking." Aunt Nor herded the kids toward the family room. "*Star Trek: Deep Space Nine* coming up."

Amber was left alone in the kitchen. Aunt Nor didn't

trust her. Well, who could blame her? Why should anybody believe what Amber said anymore?

If only she could change that.

She took her phone upstairs into the kids' bathroom and shut the door. By now, Lottie had left three voicemails. Voicemails were acts of desperation. Amber played the first one, which featured a baby wailing in the background.

"Hello from Howl's Castle." A door creaked. The crying grew fainter. "I'm inside my closet fortress. I swear James was born with the lungs of a full-grown man. Rasheeda says every baby has a fussy time but with him it's more like an I-will-dominate-the-world time. Are you there? Please pick up. No? Okay. But I miss you like...like my beleaguered ears miss silence."

Amber gathered towels off the floor and put them in the hamper. She tossed scattered bath toys into their basket, scrubbed out the sink, and replaced the empty toilet paper roll. At last she sat on the floor, leaned against the tub, and tapped Lottie's number.

"You live!" her friend cried. "Amboo, what's going on?"

"I'm going to tell you. By the end you won't want to be my friend anymore, so I'll just say right now, I wish I'd been a better friend when your mother died."

"Whaaaat?"

"Here I go."

It was shocking how few words it took to tell something so enormous. Maybe that was the difference between the truth and a made-up story. The truth just stood there, more or less naked but not caring what anybody thought, while stories wore lots of accessories. When she got to the end, Amber said she was sorry for not telling Lottie before. *I'm sorry*: words people kept saying after the fire. Words she'd heard so often, they'd quit meaning anything.

Now, it seemed, she'd be saying them herself, over and over and over.

"I'm sure Gage is fine," was the first thing Lottie said. "He just needs a break from everything. He'll come back when he's ready."

A rush of gratitude mixed with sorrow! It was so like Lottie to get the big picture. To think beyond her own personal hurt. She really was the best friend possible. *Had been* the best friend possible.

"Oh Lot," Amber whispered. "I wrecked everything."

Lottie was quiet a long moment before answering.

"I respect that Gage swore you to secrecy," she said then. "But I still wish you'd told me what was happening. I would've helped. Who knows how, considering how convoluted this all is. It would've been difficult. Possibly impossible. But I still wish you'd told me."

"I'm so stupid."

"Don't say that."

"I know I hurt you. I didn't mean to." *Stop!* Amber commanded herself. *Tell the truth!* "I mean, yes. I did. I knew I was hurting you. All the attention freaked me out at first, but then I liked it. I really liked it, Lottie, and I cared more about that than about you."

"Did you tell Mariah any of this?"

"I don't think I can. I'm not sure she'll forgive me."

"Maybe she will, but I don't exactly feel like I know her anymore." Lottie sighed. In the distance, a baby began to cry. "What did you mean? About when my mother died?"

"You were so sad all the time. At first I felt bad for you, but then I just wanted the sadness to be over. It was too scary to think that mothers could die. Or maybe...maybe it didn't even seem real to me. That something so terrible could actually happen." Amber swallowed. The bathroom floor was so cold. She drew up her knees and hugged them. "I let you down when you needed me most."

"I don't remember that."

"You don't?"

"You know what I remember? One day I was crying by the willow tree on the playground. Remember how we loved that tree? And you took a little branch and bent it into a heart."

"I did?"

"I kept it for a long time." Lottie smiled—Amber heard it in her voice.

Amber rested her chin on her knees. It seemed like nothing ever happened once. It happened again and again, depending on who told the story. But then how were you ever supposed to figure out the truth? Unless there was no single solitary truth. Unless the truth was as confusing as people, who could be good and bad, kind and selfish, brave and weak, familiar and changing, all rolled into one.

"I lost that willow heart," Lottie went on, "but I can still picture it. Some things can't ever be lost, I guess."

Was she thinking about her mother? Amber's own, real heart swelled. You couldn't truly lose the things and people you'd loved. They'd always be with you. Always be there, filling you with a longing that was sad and joyful, bitter and sweet, at the same time.

"I missed you," she told Lottie.

"Like the tundra... no, wait. Like a right triangle would miss its hypotenuse."

Lottie! Still and forever a nerd.

Amber was so glad.

Where r u?

By now it was early evening. Mom and Dad were still not back and the house was quiet except for the sounds of *Star Trek* in the family room. Amber drifted from room to room, cuddling Earrings, feeling his old rabbit heart thump in his chest. She stood by the front window, where just last night Clancy had watched for Dad's car. The street was empty now.

Homer nudged her knee. He dropped his beloved penguin stuffie, matted with dog drool, at her feet.

"Thanks," she told him, and he licked her hand. Which still held her phone. She juggled Earrings into the crook of her arm and tried again.

Where r u? please tell me no not please—tell me! U have to! We r in this together

Earrings's velvet ears flicked. Amber's phone vibrated.

Never, ever would she have guessed what her brother texted back.

Though why? By now, it should not have surprised her one bit.

Coming, she texted, and a heartbeat later, he answered.

Hurry.

Where He Was

It was easy to slip out of the house without anyone knowing.

Not so easy to know which bus to take, but as she hurried to the stop she used her phone to figure it out and—for once, life was fair and just! The bus she needed pulled up within minutes.

She got off at the nearest stop and ran the last two blocks. The building was long and low, and its windows were regular windows, no bars, thank goodness. Still. She was out of breath from running, but she would've gasped anyway when she saw the sign, which did not mince words:

POLICE.

Inside, a tall gray desk. Two wide metal doors, also gray. Exactly one gray plastic chair, in which her brother sat.

That was when she realized. All the way here, the only thing in her head was: Gage needs me. Not for one second did she wonder what she'd do when she got here. Try to stop him? Stand by him?

As she crossed the shiny gray linoleum floor, she knew.

"Hey."

"Hey."

He edged over, sharing the stingy chair. He still wore the same clothes as last night, and she could smell his salty sweat.

"This place is extremely gray," she whispered. "They need a new decorator."

"Word. How'd you get here so fast?"

"I've become a bus ninja."

They eyed the gray doors.

"Gage? Why'd you do this alone?"

"Because." He folded, unfolded, refolded his hands. "I had to. I couldn't stand Dad taking over or Mom treating me like a freaking baby, saying it was all going to be okay." He tucked his chin to his chest. "But when it came down to it, I just kept wandering around. I couldn't do it by myself after all."

She rested her head on his shoulder. "You don't have to."

One of the gray metal doors opened and an officer stepped out. She had long curly hair and a tight smile. Her uniform was gray, and menace-y type things hung from her belt.

"Gage Price, we're ready for you." When he stood up, so did Amber. The officer cocked an eyebrow.

"I'm his sister."

"And?"

"And. Where he goes, I go." Amber swallowed. "Please."

• • •

Afterward, the officer called Mom, then told them they could go for now. They stepped out into the waiting area where the single chair, amazingly, held Kelly B. Her father, tall and red-faced, loomed up beside her.

"Amber!" Kelly B. jumped up. Her eyes darted to Gage. "What are you—"

"This is no time for socializing, Kelly," Mr. B. growled. Though Kelly was the last person Amber wanted to see right now, her father's anger made Amber shiver with sympathy. He turned to the police officer. "We're here to report a stolen bike. A very expensive bike that my daughter just happened to forget to lock."

Gage was already headed for the outside door, but Kelly B. caught Amber's sleeve.

"What's going on?" she whispered. "What's up with your brother?"

"Kelly!" her father commanded. "What'd I say?"

"Sorry, Dad!" she said, but she held onto Amber a moment longer. "Text me everything! I need to know everything!"

Gage was already standing on the sidewalk. When Amber came out, he hooked an arm over her shoulder.

"When this all gets out, it's going to blow big-time for you."

She sagged against him. "For you too."

The streetlights winked on just as Dad's car zoomed around the corner. It barely came to a stop before Mom jumped out and threw her arms around Gage.

"We were so worried! What did you—? Amber, how did you—? Oh, my poor sweeties!"

"Get in," Dad said. "It's cold."

On the way to Aunt Nor's, Gage described how the police had taken a report, how they advised him not to say more without a lawyer, how they were going to question Ceecee, how the insurance agency would be informed, how the county prosecutor would decide potential charges. As he spoke, Mom kept twisting around in her seat, looking at him with a mix of disbelief and sorrow. Dad kept his eyes straight ahead, both hands on the wheel.

"I have to have a hearing in juvenile court," Gage said. "After that, it's up to the judge. I guess some are harsher than others—it's the luck of the draw."

"I can't believe you did this without us!" Mom cried. "Why didn't you let us come with you?"

"Meg." Dad's voice was stern, the way it so often was, but tonight Amber heard something new. He was being stern with himself, too. She looked at the back of his defenseless, nearly hairless head. "We both wish we'd been there," Dad said. "But Gage decided for himself."

He found Amber in the rearview mirror, and for a

moment she was afraid he'd lecture her for sneaking out, for keeping yet another secret from him. But when their gazes met, all she saw was a tender pride.

"Besides," Dad said. "He had his sister."

At Aunt Nor's there were many more exclamations and cries and hugs before she hustled all the twins upstairs. By now, it was almost time for bed.

"You must be starving," Mom told Gage. "Go sit in the family room and I'll make us all something to eat."

Outside, the moon silvered the bare branches of the trees. Gage dove onto the family room couch and dragged the lumpy afghan over his head. Amber and Clancy wriggled under it, too.

"This is nice," Clancy said. "It can be our house."

"Anyplace we're together, that's our house," Gage said.

This was one of those things people said. Things like *Material possessions don't matter* or *Every cloud has a silver lining* or *Honesty is the best policy*. Things that were easy to say without any idea what you were talking about. But now, as her brother and sister leaned against her, as she heard her parents quietly talking in the kitchen, Amber knew this saying, at least, was true.

Wherever they were together was their home.

If only she didn't have to go back to school.

Hangdog Ugly

On Monday, Amber asked Mom to drive her to school early. The halls were spookily empty. She hurried to her locker, then around the corner, past the Price of Kindness posters (When would they take them down? Please today!), up the stairs to the library. The door was locked. Amber, leaning against the wall, heard footsteps clicking toward her. Melissa Thom, in her uniform of a crisp blouse and blood-red lipstick.

"Amber! I was hoping I'd see you today."

"Erm. Hi, Melissa."

"I heard rumors about what happened."

Lots of people, not to say *everyone*, had. Even Lottie, who was usually out of the gossip loop, had told Amber that she'd heard about Kelly B. seeing them in the police station. Gage was in trouble with the law. Nobody knew exactly how, though there were plenty of theories, but he must have done *something* illegal. Why else would he act like that at the ceremony?

"I never believe rumors," Melissa said. "So I did some investigative journalism, with a little help from my dad.

Police records are public." Her professional composure showed a crack. "I'm sorry, Amber. I know this must be hard. Could we do another interview where you explain?"

"I don't think so."

"That's how you feel right now." Melissa's perfect posture had deserted her. Her shoulders sagged. "I'm saying this as a friend as well as a reporter. You need to tell your side of things. If you don't, people will just go with toxic gossip and disinformation."

Mr. Barrow was coming down the hall. His ring of keys jingled as he pulled them from his backpack and unlocked the door.

"Good morning, girls." He gave Amber a concerned-adult look. Even Mr. Barrow must have heard the rumors. "I'm guessing you'd like to come in," he said.

"Yes please." She dove into the room.

"Think it over, Amber," Melissa called after her. "I could get it online by the end of the week."

Sitting alongside the great white shark, she listened to the hallways slowly come to life. Voices calling, sneakers squeaking, locker doors slamming. The second bell rang and everything fell abruptly, eerily quiet.

Mr. Barrow asked if she'd like to go to the nurse. Or maybe the counselor.

"Please?" she whispered. "Can I just stay here for a while?"

"I'll speak to Mrs. Stefanski," the librarian said gently. He set a Clifford the Big Red Dog stuffie on the chair beside her.

Amber pulled encyclopedias off the shelf and fortressed them around her. She slid her pendant side to side.

During first period, a sixth-grade class came in to do research. Amber ducked behind the *XYZ* volume, but that didn't shield her from the whispering and snickering.

"It's her."

"What is she doing, hiding out?"

"Wouldn't you?"

"I'd move to Canada."

Mrs. Oluonye found her during third period. She didn't have her cane today, and quickly crossed the room, her beautiful red-and-purple dress swirling around her. Before she could reach Amber, two eighth graders passed the table, talking behind their hands.

"It was all a swindle."

"I heard he's getting charged with arson."

"Their family was trying to collect the insurance money? Like half a million dollars or something?"

Mrs. O. threw the eighth graders an aren't-you-supposed-to-be-somewhere-else look as she pulled out a chair across the table.

"Amber," she said. "I missed you in class."

Amber tried to speak but her voice didn't work.

"Mr. Barrow sent your teachers a message saying you needed space, and Mrs. Stefanski okayed it for today." Mrs. O. hitched her chair a little closer. "How can I help?"

"No offense," Amber managed to say. "But you can't."

"How about if you just tell me what happened?"

Amber was surprised again by how few words it took to tell the truth. Especially when the person listening paid attention to every single one of those words, making you feel the weight of each one. When Amber was finished, Mrs. O. sat back in her chair. The wrinkles around her eyes were like rings in a golden pond.

"One thing is the same," she said, her voice kinder than ever. "It doesn't change, no matter who tells this story."

"What?"

"Your brother is an extraordinarily brave boy."

"I know. I know that, upside down and inside out! But people won't see him that way now."

"How people see him—does that change the truth?"

"No. And I don't want to care what people think of us." Amber swallowed. "But I can't help it."

"You're making a mistake if you assume everyone feels the same way." Mrs. Oluonye clasped her hands on the table. "In my class you skipped? Your classmates wanted to talk about all this. You're right that some are angry, some are confused, and some—some, I'm sorry to say, are just enjoying the whole dustup."

"See? That's why I couldn't be there."

"You missed out, Amber. Eventually, our discussion got around to the notion of kindness and I asked for a definition. Not from the dictionary—from their own hearts. That turned out to be harder than anybody thought. Mei said 'Kindness is a gift you give to a person who needs it.' Everyone thought that sounded right, till Lottie said 'If it's a gift, can you change your mind and take it back? Because then it's not really a gift.' And Maxwell said 'Yeah, if only *some* people deserve kindness, then it's just a reward.'"

"Maxwell said that?"

"He did. That boy needs to stop hiding his smarts under his sneer." Mrs. Oluonye smiled. "When I retire, there are things about teaching I won't miss, but puzzling out the world alongside you children? That I will miss very, very much." The bell rang. She flattened her hands on the table and stood up. "I've spoken to Selena and Justin. They still want your family to have the money, but they know some people won't. We'll have to figure that out."

Mrs. Oluonye pushed in her chair. She picked up the *XYZ* encyclopedia and slid it back onto the shelf. She gave the Clifford stuffie a pat.

"Mrs. O.?"

"Yes?"

"No offense again, but your poster is wrong. Truth isn't beautiful. I mean, it's not even halfway nice looking."

"You're right, Amber. The truth is often hangdog ugly." Mrs. O. nodded. "But I guarantee you this. Facing the truth—that *is* always a thing of beauty. And you, my friend, you are doing that." She smiled. "I do need to change that poster, though."

"Thank you. For letting me skip."

"I did not *let* you, but since you're here and since Mrs. Stefanski okayed it, you can. Being kind to yourself is important, too. But you can't hide out forever, Amber. When you come back tomorrow, I'll be there. And not just me. You'll see."

Her teacher was right: She couldn't hide out forever. By now, she really needed to pee. She slipped down the empty hallway and had almost made it safely back to the library when she heard a familiar buzzing sound. Lucas, trumpet case in hand, rounded the corner. He froze, lips pursed.

"Hi."

"Hi."

Lucas winced like he had a cramp. Like he'd eaten something rotten. Amber rushed past him, back into the library, her heart plunging into her high-tops.

• • •

Kelly B. and Mei found her next.

"We feel like we've been used," Kelly B. said.

"I'm sorry," Amber said.

"Sorry we feel used?"

"I didn't mean that." Amber's throat closed up. What did she mean? Mei's face got puckery.

"We're sorry your brother has to go to jail," she said.

"He's having a hearing. We don't know for sure what will happen after that."

"Anyway," Kelly B. said. "We decided you've been through a lot, so we won't hold a grudge." When she smoothed her already smooth hair, Amber flashed to how furious her father had been at the police station. Kelly's life, unlike her hair and her eyebrows, was not perfect. "It won't be easy, but we plan to forgive you." Kelly paused. "Eventually."

"It's hard to be kind!" Mei blurted. "But we'll try."

Kelly B. stalked away and Mei stumbled behind her.

Amber rested her head on her folded arms. Her hair fell across her face and she didn't push it away. It was easier to cry behind a curtain. Someone went by on mouse feet. Then came back. Amber didn't dare look up. But a granola bar slid into view beside her.

"You must be hungry by now."

"Jessie." Amber had been too anxious to eat breakfast,

and the sight of the bar made her mouth water in a thoroughly humiliating way. "Thank you."

"You're welcome." And then, "I'm sorry you're hurting."

"*You* don't need to be sorry. *You're* never mean!"

"Not sorry like I did something wrong. Just sorry for how sucky life can be."

"So you're apologizing for life?"

When Jessie smiled, her eyes lit up like they held little candles. "I guess so. Something like that."

She sat at her table and Amber sat at hers. But somehow, after that, they were sitting together.

What It Means

Amber dreaded seeing Mariah all day, and Mariah must have dreaded it, too, because she never came to the library. Amber kept her phone off till she was home, when she found a text from her once-best friend: **u can keep the clothes**

Because she wanted to be nice? Or because she didn't want anything more to do with Amber?

thanx, she texted back. And then: **miss u like u know what**

She didn't want Mariah's clothes, though. They'd never felt like hers, had always made her feel like she was playing dress-up. Mariah had meant well, just like Lottie had meant well when she talked Amber into advanced math, but really? What her friends were doing was trying to make her more like themselves.

Amoeba that she was, that hadn't been hard.

Amber pulled the box of donations from the back of the hall closet and set the boots inside. Her pinched toes would thank her.

Mariah hadn't mentioned the necklace. Amber hoped that meant she could keep it. She'd come to love its tiny spark. Almost to depend on it. Looking in the mirror above the hall table, she held it up to see the insect caught inside. There it was, a zillion years old. Squinting in the mirror, she wondered if the blobbish person she'd been before was still inside her. Could she be old and new at the same time?

Nobody else can tell you who you are, Dad said. *Only you can decide that.*

You're the one who gets to decide what it all means, Aunt Nor said.

Deciding was a lonesome thing. Lonesome and scary but also, in a way, powerful.

Amber: **how about asking jessie morris to eat with us**
Lottie: **won't she say no**
Amber: **maybe**
Lottie: **k—let's ask.**

Later, Amber got three more texts.

The first one said: **can't tell if u want 2 talk**

She stared at the message. He must mean it for someone else. He'd sent it by mistake.

But then a second message: **thinking no, wishing yes**

And then a third.

Lucas: **sending solicitude (that's a real word)**

• • •

Two mornings later, as she hunted through her locker for her chorus music, she felt a sharp tap on her shoulder. Maxwell, standing too close.

"You better pray your brother gets a good judge. Some of them just want to stick it to kids. Like the one my brother got."

She wished he wasn't standing so close. She wished he didn't have something dark caught between his front teeth. But she didn't step back.

"I'm sorry." Those dumb words! But she meant them the same way Jessie had—that she wished life didn't sometimes hurt so much. She tried again. "I'm sorry for what happened to him and your family. The whole thing is so scary."

"You don't have to tell me." But he looked like he appreciated it anyway. "My brother's probably going to get out early. At least we hope."

"I hope so, too."

When he started to walk away, Amber followed.

"Before," she said, and he turned around. "Before—I didn't know how hard things can be." She fumbled to say what she meant. Something *true*. "I didn't know how things can seem not so bad, as long as they happen to other people instead of you."

He shifted his feet.

"But now I know," she said. "And I'm not going to forget."

"Yeah. That's what you say now."

"If I forget, then all this terrible stuff happened for no reason. I don't think I could stand that."

He looked at her like, maybe, possibly, he was realizing something for the first time, too. He started to walk away again, then turned.

"By the way, Lucas the Mucus is all right. Just don't tell him I said so."

"No worries."

They both grinned.

Outside her classroom, Mrs. Oluonye had hung a new Words of Wisdom poster. Amber and Maxwell stood side by side to read it:

> *Kindness is not a reward. Everybody deserves it, no matter what.*
>
> —Maxwell Driver and Lottie Jackson.

What She Saved

Even after Uncle Neither put the extensions in the dining room table, it was still barely big enough for two Thanksgiving feasts—one carnivore, one vegetarian. Beside each setting was a pretty place card Mom had made. Just as she'd promised, she was still making pretty things.

All the grown-ups were in the kitchen, even Dad who'd never, in Amber's memory, cooked anything more complicated than a fried egg. He was peeling potatoes, slowly and fastidiously. So slowly and fastidiously that Aunt Nor tapped her foot.

"We do hope to eat before midnight, Gus," she said.

"Really?" Dad said. "You could've told me that before, Noreen."

Mom shook her head. "You two!"

Aunt Nor harrumphed and carried a bowl of cranberries into the dining room. Amber trailed behind with a dish of celery and olives. Her aunt wiped her hands on her apron and sighed.

"When you move out, this table is going to be much too empty."

Mom had started looking for a new place to rent. There wouldn't be any insurance money now that they'd established the cause of the fire. Dad said they'd try to sell the house, to find a buyer who'd tear it down and rebuild on the lot. There were still so many questions to decide. Meanwhile, neither he nor Mom was saying for sure if they were getting back together.

Maybe they still weren't sure themselves.

"Aunt Nor," Amber said, "remember when you told me life can go from good to bad to good again? Or something like that?"

"That sounds like something I'd say."

"You were right. And you were right about Mom, too. She's different. I'm thinking Dad's changed, too."

Her aunt's face softened. "Maybe, babycakes. Maybe. I hope so." She wiped her eyes with the corner of her apron. "You have to promise to come stay with us on a regular basis, understand? Me and Uncle Neither, the twins, the animals, we'll never manage without you." She popped an olive into her mouth and one into Amber's, too. "Amber the anchor!"

They stood tall and Vulcan-saluted each other.

Back in the kitchen, Earrings was chomping his own holiday feast of chopped-up carrots. Homer, delirious with all the good smells, kept getting under everyone's feet.

Amber took his leash and pulled on Gage's hoodie, hanging on a hook by the door. She stuffed a poop bag into the pocket. The sun shone, but it was November-cold. Homer trotted down the sidewalk, past the blow-up turkey, past steamed-up windows and extra cars in driveways. A child, nose squished against the window, waved, and Amber waved back.

She'd gotten to know this neighborhood. Almost to feel at home. Though she'd never wanted to live here, the thought of moving again made her edges wobble. She wanted to go. She didn't want to go.

What if the only sure thing was that *nothing* was sure?

Homer chased a squirrel up a tree, where it scolded in rodent-y fury. It reminded her of what Maxwell had said about mean judges. What nobody was talking about today, what everyone was trying to forget at least for these few hours, was Gage's upcoming court hearing. The whole family was going. Ceecee too. She and her foster mother had talked to the police, and she might be charged, too. Another thing not for sure yet. What was sure was that she and Amber texted sometimes now, and Amber liked her more and more. And Gage said whatever happened next, he and Ceecee would stick it out together.

In spite of everything, when Gage told Amber this, that enormous, goofy smile took over his whole face.

Dad had tried to tell Clancy a courtroom was no place for a little kid, but she'd pitched the tantrum of her life, which was saying something. *I used to be a little kid but not anymore! Besides I have stuff to tell the judge about Gage!*

Dad caved, though he made it clear Clancy would need to keep perfectly quiet. And absolutely no musk ox helmet.

Amber, though. She was going to testify.

Her edges wobbled again. The lawyer they'd talked to said that because the fire was an accident, and because Gage had no criminal history and was so full of remorse, the punishment could be community service, but it all depended on what the judge decided. Taking the stand was Amber's idea. She wanted, with every single ounce of her being, to rescue Gage the way he'd rescued her. Yet the closer the day came, the more she worried if she'd have the courage.

She'd never be as brave as Gage. Nowhere near.

But she could try.

Homer found his favorite spot and assumed the position. Amber scooped up the mess—was that actually a chess pawn? By the time they headed back, the sun was slipping down the sky, giving them long-legged shadows. Aunt Nor's front door was propped open. From inside came a shrill, penetrating noise.

Amber froze. Did she smell smoke? Her eyes began to burn and she thought she tasted black grit. No. It couldn't be. She raced up the front walk just as Bert stepped out, waving a dish towel.

"Mom burned the potatoes," she said.

The hallway was hazy with thin gray smoke, but when Amber rushed inside everyone was there, safe and sound and laughing. Well, Aunt Nor and Dad were not exactly laughing. The back door was propped open, too, and cold fresh air was pouring in, and now the smoke detector went abruptly silent, and Dad said he'd go to the market for more potatoes, and Uncle Neither said didn't they already have enough food for the entire population of New Zealand, and Homer took the chance to grab a drumstick off the platter and make a getaway, and the little twins chased him into the backyard without any shoes on, and when Amber went into the dining room to try to catch her breath, Gage stood there by himself. She could tell—no need to beam their thoughts—he was as shaken up as she was.

Would the night of the fire always be with them? Would they carry it inside like a tiny insect trapped in honey-colored stone?

Maybe. Probably, she thought.

Dad was closing the doors against the night air. Clancy was challenging Bert to a fake-burp contest, Uncle Neither was looking for the gravy boat, Mom was wrapping buttery rolls in a napkin. The house was growing warm again, and Amber watched as her family, a family much bigger and wilder than before, gathered 'round.

Carefully, gently, she touched her brother's arm. When all you owned got snatched away, when you lost what seemed like your entire known life—when that happened, it was like you were wandering around some strange, empty stage, wearing a costume that didn't fit. You didn't know what role you were supposed to be acting. Who you were, what you were supposed to say.

But then. Then you looked again, and you saw the people who cared about you. They were sitting in the front row, leaning forward in their seats. Ears ready to listen. Hands ready to clap. Arms ready to hug.

And looking into their faces, you knew you were the same person as before, only not exactly. Because you knew what you'd lost, and that was a big thing to know.

But even bigger was knowing what you still had.

Gage looked down at her. He was healing well, the wound turning into an extremely nasty scar. Every time she saw it, she'd be reminded of their true story. As if she could ever forget. Now he fixed her with a scowl.

"You're wearing my hoodie."

"I know."

"Give it back."

"There's a sack of poop in the pocket."

"*What?*"

"I saved it for you."

"I'll save you!" he yelled.

"You already did that," Ernie said, solemnly taking her seat.

"Oh yeah, right." Gage smacked his forehead. "Big mistake."

"Can I get your attention, please?" Aunt Nor tapped a glass with a spoon. "It's time to give thanks."

She was right.

Acknowledgments

I am deeply grateful to John Hiller, RN, BSN, CCRN-CSC, Nurse Manager of the MetroHealth Burn Unit; to John Hammond, RN; and to Charles "Chuck" Sprague, retired Cuyahoga County Juvenile Court Judge. Thank you for lending this book your professional expertise and for the crucial, compassionate work you do.

Fondest thanks to my editor Margaret Ferguson, who once again helped me turn a blobby amoeba into a book, and to Kristin Ostby, my new-but-already-beloved agent.

My tireless, brilliant and *kind* early readers—Mary Grimm, Susan Grimm, Mary Norris, Kris Ohlson, Shelley Pearsall, and Paul Springstubb—where would I be without you? I can't even think!

And to the teachers, librarians, and other adults who work so hard, against ever greater challenges, to give young readers books that delight, solace, and illuminate their lives: you are truth and beauty!